The Black Mask

The Black Mask

E.W. Hornung

MINT EDITIONS

The Black Mask was first published in 1901.

This edition published by Mint Editions 2021.

ISBN 9781513280646 | E-ISBN 9781513285665

Published by Mint Editions®

MINT
EDITIONS

minteditionbooks.com

Publishing Director: Jennifer Newens
Design & Production: Rachel Lopez Metzger
Project Manager: Micaela Clark
Typesetting: Westchester Publishing Services

Contents

No Sinecure

I

I AM STILL UNCERTAIN WHICH surprised me more, the telegram calling my attention to the advertisement, or the advertisement itself. The telegram is before me as I write. It would appear to have been handed in at Vere Street at eight o'clock in the morning of May 11, 1897, and received before half-past at Holloway B.O. And in that drab region it duly found me, unwashen but at work before the day grew hot and my attic insupportable.

"See Mr. Maturin's advertisement Daily Mail might suit you earnestly beg try will speak if necessary——"

I transcribe the thing as I see it before me, all in one breath that took away mine; but I leave out the initials at the end, which completed the surprise. They stood very obviously for the knighted specialist whose consulting-room is within a cab-whistle of Vere Street, and who once called me kinsman for his sins. More recently he had called me other names. I was a disgrace, qualified by an adjective which seemed to me another. I had made my bed, and I could go and lie and die in it. If I ever again had the insolence to show my nose in that house, I should go out quicker than I came in. All this, and more, my least distant relative could tell a poor devil to his face; could ring for his man, and give him his brutal instructions on the spot; and then relent to the tune of this telegram! I have no phrase for my amazement. I literally could not believe my eyes. Yet their evidence was more and more conclusive: a very epistle could not have been more characteristic of its sender. Meanly elliptical, ludicrously precise, saving half-pence at the expense of sense, yet paying like a man for "Mr." Maturin, that was my distinguished relative from his bald patch to his corns. Nor was all the rest unlike him, upon second thoughts. He had a reputation for charity; he was going to live up to it after all. Either that, or it was the sudden impulse of which the most calculating are capable at times; the morning papers with the early cup of tea, this advertisement seen by chance, and the rest upon the spur of a guilty conscience.

Well, I must see it for myself, and the sooner the better, though work pressed. I was writing a series of articles upon prison life, and had my nib into the whole System; a literary and philanthropical daily was parading my "charges," the graver ones with the more gusto; and the terms, if unhandsome for creative work, were temporary wealth to me. It so happened that my first check had just arrived by the eight o'clock post; and my position should be appreciated when I say that I had to cash it to obtain a Daily Mail.

Of the advertisement itself, what is to be said? It should speak for itself if I could find it, but I cannot, and only remember that it was a "male nurse and constant attendant" that was "wanted for an elderly gentleman in feeble health." A male nurse! An absurd tag was appended, offering "liberal salary to University or public-school man"; and of a sudden I saw that I should get this thing if I applied for it. What other "University or public-school man" would dream of doing so? Was any other in such straits as I? And then my relenting relative; he not only promised to speak for me, but was the very man to do so. Could any recommendation compete with his in the matter of a male nurse? And need the duties of such be necessarily loathsome and repellent? Certainly the surroundings would be better than those of my common lodging-house and own particular garret; and the food; and every other condition of life that I could think of on my way back to that unsavory asylum. So I dived into a pawnbroker's shop, where I was a stranger only upon my present errand, and within the hour was airing a decent if antiquated suit, but little corrupted by the pawnbroker's moth, and a new straw hat, on the top of a tram.

The address given in the advertisement was that of a flat at Earl's Court, which cost me a cross-country journey, finishing with the District Railway and a seven minutes' walk. It was now past mid-day, and the tarry wood-pavement was good to smell as I strode up the Earl's Court Road. It was great to walk the civilized world again. Here were men with coats on their backs, and ladies in gloves. My only fear was lest I might run up against one or other whom I had known of old. But it was my lucky day. I felt it in my bones. I was going to get this berth; and sometimes I should be able to smell the wood-pavement on the old boy's errands; perhaps he would insist on skimming over it in his bath-chair, with me behind.

I felt quite nervous when I reached the flats. They were a small pile in a side street, and I pitied the doctor whose plate I saw upon the palings before the ground-floor windows; he must be in a very small way, I thought. I rather pitied myself as well. I had indulged in visions of better flats than these. There were no balconies. The porter was out of livery. There was no lift, and my invalid on the third floor! I trudged up, wishing I had never lived in Mount Street, and brushed against a dejected individual coming down. A full-blooded young fellow in a frock-coat flung the right door open at my summons.

"Does Mr. Maturin live here?" I inquired.

"That's right," said the full-blooded young man, grinning all over a convivial countenance.

"I—I've come about his advertisement in the Daily Mail."

"You're the thirty-ninth," cried the blood; "that was the thirty-eighth you met upon the stairs, and the day's still young. Excuse my staring at you. Yes, you pass your prelim., and can come inside; you're one of the few. We had most just after breakfast, but now the porter's heading off the worst cases, and that last chap was the first for twenty minutes. Come in here."

And I was ushered into an empty room with a good bay-window, which enabled my full-blooded friend to inspect me yet more critically in a good light; this he did without the least false delicacy; then his questions began.

"Varsity man?"

"No."

"Public school?"

"Yes."

"Which one?"

I told him, and he sighed relief.

"At last! You're the very first I've not had to argue with as to what is and what is not a public school. Expelled?"

"No," I said, after a moment's hesitation; "no, I was not expelled. And I hope you won't expel me if I ask a question in my turn?"

"Certainly not."

"Are you Mr. Maturin's son?"

"No, my name's Theobald. You may have seen it down below."

"The doctor?" I said.

"His doctor," said Theobald, with a satisfied eye. "Mr. Maturin's doctor. He is having a male nurse and attendant by my advice, and he wants a gentleman if he can get one. I rather think he'll see you, though he's only seen two or three all day. There are certain questions which he prefers to ask himself, and it's no good going over the same ground twice. So perhaps I had better tell him about you before we get any further."

And he withdrew to a room still nearer the entrance, as I could hear, for it was a very small flat indeed. But now two doors were shut between us, and I had to rest content with murmurs through the wall until the doctor returned to summon me.

"I have persuaded my patient to see you," he whispered, "but I confess I am not sanguine of the result. He is very difficult to please. You must prepare yourself for a querulous invalid, and for no sinecure if you get the billet."

"May I ask what's the matter with him?"

"By all means—when you've got the billet."

Dr. Theobald then led the way, his professional dignity so thoroughly intact that I could not but smile as I followed his swinging coat-tails to the sick-room. I carried no smile across the threshold of a darkened chamber which reeked of drugs and twinkled with medicine bottles, and in the middle of which a gaunt figure lay abed in the half-light.

"Take him to the window, take him to the window," a thin voice snapped, "and let's have a look at him. Open the blind a bit. Not as much as that, damn you, not as much as that!"

The doctor took the oath as though it had been a fee. I no longer pitied him. It was now very clear to me that he had one patient who was a little practice in himself. I determined there and then that he should prove a little profession to me, if we could but keep him alive between us. Mr. Maturin, however, had the whitest face that I have ever seen, and his teeth gleamed out through the dusk as though the withered lips no longer met about them; nor did they except in speech; and anything ghastlier than the perpetual grin of his repose I defy you to imagine. It was with this grin that he lay regarding me while the doctor held the blind.

"So you think you could look after me, do you?"

"I'm certain I could, sir."

"Single-handed, mind! I don't keep another soul. You would have to cook your own grub and my slops. Do you think you could do all that?"

"Yes, sir, I think so."

"Why do you? Have you any experience of the kind?"

"No, sir, none."

"Then why do you pretend you have?"

"I only meant that I would do my best."

"Only meant, only meant! Have you done your best at everything else, then?"

I hung my head. This was a facer. And there was something in my invalid which thrust the unspoken lie down my throat.

"No, sir, I have not," I told him plainly.

"He, he, he!" the old wretch tittered; "and you do well to own it; you do well, sir, very well indeed. If you hadn't owned up, out you would have gone, out neck-and-crop! You've saved your bacon. You may do more. So you are a public-school boy, and a very good school yours is, but you weren't at either University. Is that correct?"

"Absolutely."

"What did you do when you left school?"

"I came in for money."

"And then?"

"I spent my money."

"And since then?"

I stood like a mule.

"And since then, I say!"

"A relative of mine will tell you if you ask him. He is an eminent man, and he has promised to speak for me. I would rather say no more myself."

"But you shall, sir, but you shall! Do you suppose that I suppose a public-school boy would apply for a berth like this if something or other hadn't happened? What I want is a gentleman of sorts, and I don't much care what sort; but you've got to tell me what did happen, if you don't tell anybody else. Dr. Theobald, sir, you can go to the devil if you won't take a hint. This man may do or he may not. You have no more to say to it till I send him down to tell you one thing or the other. Clear out, sir, clear out; and if you think you've anything to complain of, you stick it down in the bill!"

In the mild excitement of our interview the thin voice had gathered strength, and the last shrill insult was screamed after the devoted medico, as he retired in such order that I felt certain he was going to take this trying patient at his word. The bedroom door closed, then the outer one, and the doctor's heels went drumming down the common stair. I was alone in the flat with this highly singular and rather terrible old man.

"And a damned good riddance!" croaked the invalid, raising himself on one elbow without delay. "I may not have much body left to boast about, but at least I've got a lost old soul to call my own. That's why I want a gentleman of sorts about me. I've been too dependent on that chap. He won't even let me smoke, and he's been in the flat all day to see I didn't. You'll find the cigarettes behind the Madonna of the Chair."

It was a steel engraving of the great Raffaelle, and the frame was tilted from the wall; at a touch a packet of cigarettes tumbled down from behind.

"Thanks; and now a light."

I struck the match and held it, while the invalid inhaled with normal lips; and suddenly I sighed. I was irresistibly reminded of my poor dear old Raffles. A smoke-ring worthy of the great A. J. was floating upward from the sick man's lips.

"And now take one yourself. I have smoked more poisonous cigarettes. But even these are not Sullivans!"

I cannot repeat what I said. I have no idea what I did. I only know—I only knew—that it was A. J. Raffles in the flesh!

II

"Yes, Bunny, it was the very devil of a swim; but I defy you to sink in the Mediterranean. That sunset saved me. The sea was on fire. I hardly swam under water at all, but went all I knew for the sun itself; when it set I must have been a mile away; until it did I was the invisible man. I figured on that, and only hope it wasn't set down as a case of suicide. I shall get outed quite soon enough, Bunny, but I'd rather be dropped by the hangman than throw my own wicket away."

"Oh, my dear old chap, to think of having you by the hand again! I feel as though we were both aboard that German liner, and all that's happened since a nightmare. I thought that time was the last!"

"It looked rather like it, Bunny. It was taking all the risks, and hitting at everything. But the game came off, and some day I'll tell you how."

"Oh, I'm in no hurry to hear. It's enough for me to see you lying there. I don't want to know how you came there, or why, though I fear you must be pretty bad. I must have a good look at you before I let you speak another word!"

I raised one of the blinds, I sat upon the bed, and I had that look. It left me all unable to conjecture his true state of health, but quite certain in my own mind that my dear Raffles was not and never would be the man that he had been. He had aged twenty years; he looked fifty at the very least. His hair was white; there was no trick about that; and his face was another white. The lines about the corners of the eyes and mouth were both many and deep. On the other hand, the eyes themselves were alight and alert as ever; they were still keen and gray and gleaming, like finely tempered steel. Even the mouth, with a cigarette to close it, was the mouth of Raffles and no other: strong and unscrupulous as the man himself. It was only the physical strength which appeared to have departed; but that was quite sufficient to make my heart bleed for the dear rascal who had cost me every tie I valued but the tie between us two.

"Think I look much older?" he asked at length.

"A bit," I admitted. "But it is chiefly your hair."

"Whereby hangs a tale for when we've talked ourselves out, though I have often thought it was that long swim that started it. Still, the Island of Elba is a rummy show, I can assure you. And Naples is a rummier!"

"You went there after all?"

"Rather! It's the European paradise for such as our noble selves. But there's no place that's a patch on little London as a non-conductor of heat; it never need get too hot for a fellow here; if it does it's his own fault. It's the kind of wicket you don't get out on, unless you get yourself out. So here I am again, and have been for the last six weeks. And I mean to have another knock."

"But surely, old fellow, you're not awfully fit, are you?"

"Fit? My dear Bunny, I'm dead—I'm at the bottom of the sea—and don't you forget it for a minute."

"But are you all right, or are you not?"

"No, I'm half-poisoned by Theobald's prescriptions and putrid cigarettes, and as weak as a cat from lying in bed."

"Then why on earth lie in bed, Raffles?"

"Because it's better than lying in gaol, as I am afraid You know, my poor dear fellow. I tell you I am dead; and my one terror is of coming to life again by accident. Can't you see? I simply dare not show my nose out of doors—by day. You have no idea of the number of perfectly innocent things a dead man daren't do. I can't even smoke Sullivans, because no one man was ever so partial to them as I was in my lifetime, and you never know when you may start a clew."

"What brought you to these mansions?"

"I fancied a flat, and a man recommended these on the boat; such a good chap, Bunny; he was my reference when it came to signing the lease. You see I landed on a stretcher—most pathetic case—old Australian without a friend in old country—ordered Engadine as last chance—no go—not an earthly—sentimental wish to die in London—that's the history of Mr. Maturin. If it doesn't hit you hard, Bunny, you're the first. But it hit friend Theobald hardest of all. I'm an income to him. I believe he's going to marry on me."

"Does he guess there's nothing wrong?"

"Knows, bless you! But he doesn't know I know he knows, and there isn't a disease in the dictionary that he hasn't treated me for since he's had me in hand. To do him justice, I believe he thinks me a hypochondriac of the first water; but that young man will go far if he keeps on the wicket. He has spent half his nights up here, at guineas apiece."

"Guineas must be plentiful, old chap!"

"They have been, Bunny. I can't say more. But I don't see why they shouldn't be again."

I was not going to inquire where the guineas came from. As if I cared! But I did ask old Raffles how in the world he had got upon my tracks; and thereby drew the sort of smile with which old gentlemen rub their hands, and old ladies nod their noses. Raffles merely produced a perfect oval of blue smoke before replying.

"I was waiting for you to ask that, Bunny; it's a long time since I did anything upon which I plume myself more. Of course, in the first place, I spotted you at once by these prison articles; they were not signed, but the fist was the fist of my sitting rabbit!"

"But who gave you my address?"

"I wheedled it out of your excellent editor; called on him at dead of night, when I occasionally go afield like other ghosts, and wept it out of him in five minutes. I was your only relative; your name was not your own name; if he insisted I would give him mine. He didn't insist, Bunny, and I danced down his stairs with your address in my pocket."

"Last night?"

"No, last week."

"And so the advertisement was yours, as well as the telegram!"

I had, of course, forgotten both in the high excitement of the hour, or I should scarcely have announced my belated discovery with such an air. As it was I made Raffles look at me as I had known him look before, and the droop of his eyelids began to sting.

"Why all this subtlety?" I petulantly exclaimed. "Why couldn't you come straight away to me in a cab?"

He did not inform me that I was hopeless as ever. He did not address me as his good rabbit.

He was silent for a time, and then spoke in a tone which made me ashamed of mine.

"You see, there are two or three of me now, Bunny: one's at the bottom of the Mediterranean, and one's an old Australian desirous of dying in the old country, but in no immediate danger of dying anywhere. The old Australian doesn't know a soul in town; he's got to be consistent, or he's done. This sitter Theobald is his only friend, and has seen rather too much of him; ordinary dust won't do for his eyes. Begin to see? To pick you out of a crowd, that was the game; to let old Theobald help to pick you, better still! To start with, he was dead against my having anybody at all; wanted me all to himself, naturally; but anything rather than kill the goose! So he is to have a fiver a week while he keeps me alive, and he's going to be married next month. That's a pity in some ways, but a good thing in others; he will want more money than he foresees, and he may always be of use to us at a pinch. Meanwhile he eats out of my hand."

I complimented Raffles on the mere composition of his telegram, with half the characteristics of my distinguished kinsman squeezed into a dozen odd words; and let him know how the old ruffian had really treated me. Raffles was not surprised; we had dined together at my relative's in the old days, and filed for reference a professional valuation of his household gods. I now learnt that the telegram had been posted, with the hour marked for its despatch, at the pillar nearest Vere Street, on the night before the advertisement was due to appear in the Daily Mail. This also had been carefully prearranged; and Raffles's only fear had been lest it might be held over despite his explicit instructions, and so drive me to the doctor for an explanation of his telegram. But the adverse chances had been weeded out and weeded out to the irreducible minimum of risk.

His greatest risk, according to Raffles, lay nearest home: bedridden invalid that he was supposed to be, his nightly terror was of running into Theobald's arms in the immediate neighborhood of the flat. But Raffles had characteristic methods of minimizing even that danger, of which something anon; meanwhile he recounted more than one of his nocturnal adventures, all, however, of a singularly innocent type; and one thing I noticed while he talked. His room was the first as you entered the flat. The long inner wall divided the room not merely from the passage but from the outer landing as well. Thus every step upon the bare stone stairs could be heard by Raffles where he lay; and he would never speak while one was ascending, until it had passed his door. The afternoon brought more than one applicant for the post which it was my duty to tell them that I had already obtained. Between three and four, however, Raffles, suddenly looking at his watch, packed me off in a hurry to the other end of London for my things.

"I'm afraid you must be famishing, Bunny. It's a fact that I eat very little, and that at odd hours, but I ought not to have forgotten you. Get yourself a snack outside, but not a square meal if you can resist one. We've got to celebrate this day this night!"

"To-night?" I cried.

"To-night at eleven, and Kellner's the place. You may well open your eyes, but we didn't go there much, if you remember, and the staff seems changed. Anyway we'll risk it for once. I was in last night, talking like a stage American, and supper's ordered for eleven sharp."

"You made as sure of me as all that!"

"There was no harm in ordering supper. We shall have it in a private room, but you may as well dress if you've got the duds."

"They're at my only forgiving relative's."

"How much will get them out, and square you up, and bring you back bag and baggage in good time?"

I had to calculate.

"A tenner, easily."

"I had one ready for you. Here it is, and I wouldn't lose any time if I were you. On the way you might look up Theobald, tell him you've got it and how long you'll be gone, and that I can't be left alone all the time. And, by Jove, yes! You get me a stall for the Lyceum at the nearest agent's; there are two or three in High Street; and say it was given you when you come in. That young man shall be out of the way to-night."

I found our doctor in a minute consulting-room and his shirt-sleeves, a tall tumbler at his elbow; at least I caught sight of the tumbler on entering; thereafter he stood in front of it, with a futility which had my sympathy.

"So you've got the billet," said Dr. Theobald. "Well, as I told you before, and as you have since probably discovered for yourself, you won't find it exactly a sinecure. My own part of the business is by no means that; indeed, there are those who would throw up the case, after the kind of treatment that you have seen for yourself. But professional considerations are not the only ones, and one cannot make too many allowances in such a case."

E.W. HORNUNG

"But what is the case?" I asked him. "You said you would tell me if I was successful."

Dr. Theobald's shrug was worthy of the profession he seemed destined to adorn; it was not incompatible with any construction which one chose to put upon it. Next moment he had stiffened. I suppose I still spoke more or less like a gentleman. Yet, after all, I was only the male nurse. He seemed to remember this suddenly, and he took occasion to remind me of the fact.

"Ah," said he, "that was before I knew you were altogether without experience; and I must say that I was surprised even at Mr. Maturin's engaging you after that; but it will depend upon yourself how long I allow him to persist in so curious an experiment. As for what is the matter with him, my good fellow, it is no use my giving you an answer which would be double Dutch to you; moreover, I have still to test your discretionary powers. I may say, however, that that poor gentleman presents at once the most complex and most troublesome case, which is responsibility enough without certain features which make it all but insupportable. Beyond this I must refuse to discuss my patient for the present; but I shall certainly go up if I can find time."

He went up within five minutes. I found him there on my return at dusk. But he did not refuse my stall for the Lyceum, which Raffles would not allow me to use myself, and presented to him off-hand without my leave.

"And don't you bother any more about me till to-morrow," snapped the high thin voice as he was off. "I can send for you now when I want you, and I'm hoping to have a decent night for once."

III

It was half-past ten when we left the flat, in an interval of silence on the noisy stairs. The silence was unbroken by our wary feet. Yet for me a surprise was in store upon the very landing. Instead of going downstairs, Raffles led me up two flights, and so out upon a perfectly flat roof.

"There are two entrances to these mansions," he explained between stars and chimney-stacks: "one to our staircase, and another round the corner. But there's only one porter, and he lives on the basement underneath us, and affects the door nearest home. We miss him by using the wrong stairs, and we run less risk of old Theobald. I got the tip from the postmen, who come up one way and down the other. Now, follow me, and look out!"

There was indeed some necessity for caution, for each half of the building had its L-shaped well dropping sheer to the base, the parapets so low that one might easily have tripped over them into eternity. However, we were soon upon the second staircase, which opened on the roof like the first. And twenty minutes of the next twenty-five we spent in an admirable hansom, skimming east.

"Not much change in the old hole, Bunny. More of these magic-lantern advertisements. . . and absolutely the worst bit of taste in town, though it's saying something, in that equestrian statue with the gilt stirrups and fixings; why don't they black the buffer's boots and his horse's hoofs while they are about it? . . . More bicyclists, of course. That was just beginning, if you remember. It might have been useful to us. . . And there's the old club, getting put into a crate for the Jubilee; by Jove, Bunny, we ought to be there. I wouldn't lean forward in Piccadilly, old chap. If you're seen I'm thought of, and we shall have to be jolly careful at Kellner's. . . Ah, there it is! Did I tell you I was a low-down stage Yankee at Kellner's? You'd better be another, while the waiter's in the room."

We had the little room upstairs; and on the very threshold I, even I, who knew my Raffles of old, was taken horribly aback. The table was laid for three. I called his attention to it in a whisper.

"Why, yep!" came through his nose. "Say, boy, the lady, she's not comin', but you leave that tackle where 'tis. If I'm liable to pay, I guess I'll have all there is to it."

I have never been in America, and the American public is the last on earth that I desire to insult; but idiom and intonation alike would have imposed upon my inexperience. I had to look at Raffles to make sure that it was he who spoke, and I had my own reasons for looking hard.

"Who on earth was the lady?" I inquired aghast at the first opportunity.

"She isn't on earth. They don't like wasting this room on two, that's all. Bunny—my Bunny—here's to us both!"

And we clinked glasses swimming with the liquid gold of Steinberg, 1868; but of the rare delights of that supper I can scarcely trust myself to write. It was no mere meal, it was no coarse orgy, but a little feast for the fastidious gods, not unworthy of Lucullus at his worst. And I who had bolted my skilly at Wormwood Scrubbs, and tightened my belt in a Holloway attic, it was I who sat down to this ineffable repast!

Where the courses were few, but each a triumph of its kind, it would be invidious to single out any one dish; but the Jambon de Westphalie au Champagne tempts me sorely. And then the champagne that we drank, not the quantity but the quality! Well, it was Pol Roger, '84, and quite good enough for me; but even so it was not more dry, nor did it sparkle more, than the merry rascal who had dragged me thus far to the devil, but should lead me dancing the rest of the way. I was beginning to tell him so. I had done my honest best since my reappearance in the world; but the world had done its worst by me. A further antithesis and my final intention were both upon my tongue when the waiter with the Chateau Margaux cut me short; for he was the bearer of more than that great wine; bringing also a card upon a silver tray.

"Show him up," said Raffles, laconically.

"And who is this?" I cried when the man was gone. Raffles reached across the table and gripped my arm in a vice. His eyes were steel points fixed on mine.

"Bunny, stand by me," said he in the old irresistible voice, a voice both stern and winning. "Stand by me, Bunny—if there's a row!"

And there was time for nothing more, the door flying open, and a dapper person entering with a bow; a frock-coat on his back, gold pince-nez on his nose; a shiny hat in one hand, and a black bag in the other.

"Good-evening, gentlemen," said he, at home and smiling.

"Sit down," drawled Raffles in casual response. "Say, let me introduce you to Mr. Ezra B. Martin, of Shicawgo. Mr. Martin is my future brother-in-law. This is Mr. Robinson, Ezra, manager to Sparks & Company, the cellerbrated joolers on Re-gent Street."

I pricked up my ears, but contented myself with a nod. I altogether distrusted my ability to live up to my new name and address.

"I figured on Miss Martin bein' right here, too," continued Raffles, "but I regret to say she's not feelin' so good. We light out for Parrus on the 9 A.M. train to-morrer mornin', and she guessed she'd be too dead. Sorry to disappoint you, Mr. Robinson; but you'll see I'm advertisin' your wares."

Raffles held his right hand under the electric light, and a diamond ring flashed upon his little finger. I could have sworn it was not there five minutes before.

The tradesman had a disappointed face, but for a moment it brightened as he expatiated on the value of that ring and on the price his people had accepted for it. I was invited to guess the figure, but I shook a discreet head. I have seldom been more taciturn in my life.

"Forty-five pounds," cried the jeweller; "and it would be cheap at fifty guineas."

"That's right," assented Raffles. "That'd be dead cheap, I allow. But then, my boy, you gotten ready cash, and don't you forget it."

I do not dwell upon my own mystification in all this. I merely pause to state that I was keenly enjoying that very element. Nothing could have been more typical of Raffles and the past. It was only my own attitude that was changed.

It appeared that the mythical lady, my sister, had just become engaged to Raffles, who seemed all anxiety to pin her down with gifts of price. I could not quite gather whose gift to whom was the diamond ring; but it had evidently been paid for; and I voyaged to the moon, wondering when and how. I was recalled to this planet by a deluge of gems from the jeweller's bag. They lay alight in their cases like the electric lamps above. We all three put our heads together over them, myself without the slightest clew as to what was coming, but not unprepared for violent crime. One does not do eighteen months for nothing.

"Right away," Raffles was saying. "We'll choose for her, and you'll change anything she don't like. Is that the idea?"

"That was my suggestion, sir."

"Then come on, Ezra. I guess you know Sadie's taste. You help me choose."

And we chose—lord! What did we not choose? There was her ring, a diamond half-hoop. It cost £95, and there was no attempt to get it for £90. Then there was a diamond necklet—two hundred guineas, but pounds accepted. That was to be the gift of the bridegroom. The wedding was evidently imminent. It behooved me to play a brotherly part. I therefore rose to the occasion; calculated she would like a diamond star (£116), but reckoned it was more than I could afford; and sustained a vicious kick under the table for either verb. I was afraid to open my mouth on finally obtaining the star for the round hundred. And then the fat fell in the fire; for pay we could not; though a remittance (said Raffles) was "overdo from Noo York."

"But I don't know you, gentlemen," the jeweller exclaimed. "I haven't even the name of your hotel!"

"I told you we was stoppin' with friends," said Raffles, who was not angry, though thwarted and crushed. "But that's right, sir! Oh, that's dead right, and I'm the last man to ask you to take Quixotic risks. I'm tryin' to figure a way out. Yes, Sir, that's what I'm tryin' to do."

"I wish you could, sir," the jeweller said, with feeling. "It isn't as if we hadn't seen the color of your money. But certain rules I'm sworn to observe; it isn't as if I was in business for myself; and—you say you start for Paris in the morning!"

"On the 9 A. M. train," mused Raffles; "and I've heard no-end yarns about the joolers' stores in Parrus. But that ain't fair; don't you take no notice o' that. I'm tryin' to figure a way out. Yes, Sir!"

He was smoking cigarettes out of a twenty-five box; the tradesman and I had cigars. Raffles sat frowning with a pregnant eye, and it was only too clear to me that his plans had miscarried. I could not help thinking, however, that they deserved to do so, if he had counted upon buying credit for all but £400 by a single payment of some ten per cent. That again seemed unworthy of Raffles, and I, for my part, still sat prepared to spring any moment at our visitor's throat.

"We could mail you the money from Parrus," drawled Raffles at length. "But how should we know you'd hold up your end of the string, and mail us the same articles we've selected to-night?"

The visitor stiffened in his chair. The name of his firm should be sufficient guarantee for that.

"I guess I'm no better acquainted with their name than they are with mine," remarked Raffles, laughing. "See here, though! I got a scheme. You pack 'em in this!"

He turned the cigarettes out of the tin box, while the jeweller and I joined wondering eyes.

"Pack 'em in this," repeated Raffles, "the three things we want, and never mind the boxes; you can pack 'em in cotton-wool. Then we'll ring for string and sealing wax, seal up the lot right here, and you can take 'em away in your grip. Within three days we'll have our remittance, and mail you the money, and you'll mail us this darned box with my seal unbroken! It's no use you lookin' so sick, Mr. Jooler; you won't trust us any, and yet we're goin' to trust you some. Ring the bell, Ezra, and we'll see if they've gotten any sealing-wax and string."

They had; and the thing was done. The tradesman did not like it; the precaution was absolutely unnecessary; but since he was taking all his goods away with him, the sold with the unsold, his sentimental objections soon fell to the ground. He packed necklet, ring, and star, with his own hands, in cotton-wool; and the cigarette-box held them so easily that at the last moment, when the box was closed, and the string ready, Raffles very nearly added a diamond bee-brooch at £51 10s. This temptation, however, he ultimately overcame, to the other's chagrin. The cigarette-box was tied up, and the string sealed, oddly enough, with the diamond of the ring that had been bought and paid for.

"I'll chance you having another ring in the store the dead spit of mine," laughed Raffles, as he relinquished the box, and it disappeared into the tradesman's bag. "And now, Mr. Robinson, I hope you'll appreciate my true hospitality in not offering you any thing to drink while business was in progress. That's Chateau Margaux, sir, and I should judge it's what you'd call an eighteen-carat article."

In the cab which we took to the vicinity of the flat, I was instantly snubbed for asking questions which the driver might easily overhear, and took the repulse just a little to heart. I could make neither head nor tail of Raffles's dealings with the man from Regent Street, and was naturally inquisitive as to the meaning of it all. But I held my tongue until we had regained the flat in the cautious manner of our exit, and even there until Raffles rallied me with a hand on either shoulder and an old smile upon his face.

"You rabbit!" said he. "Why couldn't you wait till we got home?"

"Why couldn't you tell me what you were going to do?" I retorted as of yore.

"Because your dear old phiz is still worth its weight in innocence, and because you never could act for nuts! You looked as puzzled as the other poor devil; but you wouldn't if you had known what my game really was."

"And pray what was it?"

"That," said Raffles, and he smacked the cigarette-box down upon the mantelpiece. It was not tied. It was not sealed. It flew open from the force of the impact. And the diamond ring that cost £95, the necklet for £200, and my flaming star at another £100, all three lay safe and snug in the jeweller's own cotton-wool!

"Duplicate boxes!" I cried.

"Duplicate boxes, my brainy Bunny. One was already packed and weighted, and in my pocket. I don't know whether you noticed me weighing the three things together in my hand? I know that neither of you saw me change the boxes, for I did it when I was nearest buying the bee-brooch at the end, and you were too puzzled, and the other Johnny too keen. It was the cheapest shot in the game; the dear ones

E.W. HORNUNG

were sending old Theobald to Southampton on a fool's errand yesterday afternoon, and showing one's own nose down Regent Street in broad daylight while he was gone; but some things are worth paying for, and certain risks one must always take. Nice boxes, aren't they? I only wished they contained a better cigarette; but a notorious brand was essential; a box of Sullivans would have brought me to life to-morrow."

"But they oughtn't to open it to-morrow."

"Nor will they, as a matter of fact. Meanwhile, Bunny, I may call upon you to dispose of the boodle."

"I'm on for any mortal thing!"

My voice rang true, I swear, but it was the way of Raffles to take the evidence of as many senses as possible. I felt the cold steel of his eyes through mine and through my brain. But what he saw seemed to satisfy him no less than what he heard, for his hand found my hand, and pressed it with a fervor foreign to the man.

"I know you are, and I knew you would be. Only remember, Bunny, it's my turn next to pay the shot!"

You shall hear how he paid it when the time came.

A Jubilee Present

The Room of Gold, in the British Museum, is probably well enough known to the inquiring alien and the travelled American. A true Londoner, however, I myself had never heard of it until Raffles casually proposed a raid.

"The older I grow, Bunny, the less I think of your so-called precious stones. When did they ever bring in half their market value in L.s.d. There was the first little crib we ever cracked together—you with your innocent eyes shut. A thousand pounds that stuff was worth; but how many hundreds did it actually fetch. The Ardagh emeralds weren't much better; old Lady Melrose's necklace was far worse; but that little lot the other night has about finished me. A cool hundred for goods priced well over four; and £35 to come off for bait, since we only got a tenner for the ring I bought and paid for like an ass. I'll be shot if I ever touch a diamond again! Not if it was the Koh-I-noor; those few whacking stones are too well known, and to cut them up is to decrease their value by arithmetical retrogression. Besides, that brings you up against the Fence once more, and I'm done with the beggars for good and all. You talk about your editors and publishers, you literary swine. Barabbas was neither a robber nor a publisher, but a six-barred, barbed-wired, spike-topped Fence. What we really want is an Incorporated Society of Thieves, with some public-spirited old forger to run it for us on business lines."

Raffles uttered these blasphemies under his breath, not, I am afraid, out of any respect for my one redeeming profession, but because we were taking a midnight airing on the roof, after a whole day of June in the little flat below. The stars shone overhead, the lights of London underneath, and between the lips of Raffles a cigarette of the old and only brand. I had sent in secret for a box of the best; the boon had arrived that night; and the foregoing speech was the first result. I could afford to ignore the insolent asides, however, where the apparent contention was so manifestly unsound.

"And how are you going to get rid of your gold?" said I, pertinently.

"Nothing easier, my dear rabbit."

"Is your Room of Gold a roomful of sovereigns?"

Raffles laughed softly at my scorn.

"No, Bunny, it's principally in the shape of archaic ornaments, whose value, I admit, is largely extrinsic. But gold is gold, from Phoenicia to Klondike, and if we cleared the room we should eventually do very well."

"How?"

"I should melt it down into a nugget, and bring it home from the U.S.A. to-morrow."

"And then?"

"Make them pay up in hard cash across the counter of the Bank of England. And you CAN make them."

That I knew, and so said nothing for a time, remaining a hostile though a silent critic, while we paced the cool black leads with our bare feet, softly as cats.

"And how do you propose to get enough away," at length I asked, "to make it worth while?"

"Ah, there you have it," said Raffles. "I only propose to reconnoitre the ground, to see what we can see. We might find some hiding-place for a night; that, I am afraid, would be our only chance."

"Have you ever been there before?"

"Not since they got the one good, portable piece which I believe that they exhibit now. It's a long time since I read of it—I can't remember where—but I know they have got a gold cup of sorts worth several thousands. A number of the immorally rich clubbed together and presented it to the nation; and two of the richly immoral intend to snaffle it for themselves. At any rate we might go and have a look at it, Bunny, don't you think?"

Think! I seized his arm.

"When? When? When?" I asked, like a quick-firing gun.

"The sooner the better, while old Theobald's away on his honeymoon."

Our medico had married the week before, nor was any fellow-practitioner taking his work—at least not that considerable branch of it which consisted of Raffles—during his brief absence from town. There were reasons, delightfully obvious to us, why such a plan would have been highly unwise in Dr. Theobald. I, however, was sending him daily screeds, and both matutinal and nocturnal telegrams, the composition of which afforded Raffles not a little enjoyment.

"Well, then, when—when?" I began to repeat.

"To-morrow, if you like."

"Only to look?"

The limitation was my one regret.

"We must do so, Bunny, before we leap."

"Very well," I sighed. "But to-morrow it is!"

And the morrow it really was.

I saw the porter that night, and, I still think, bought his absolute allegiance for the second coin of the realm. My story, however, invented by Raffles, was sufficiently specious in itself. That sick gentleman, Mr. Maturin (as I had to remember to call him), was really, or apparently, sickening for fresh air. Dr. Theobald would allow him none; he was pestering me for just one day in the country while the glorious weather lasted. I was myself convinced that no possible harm could come of the experiment. Would the porter help me in so innocent and meritorious an intrigue? The man hesitated. I produced my half-sovereign. The man was lost. And at half-past eight next morning—before the heat of the day—Raffles and I drove to Kew Gardens in a hired landau which was to call for us at mid-day and wait until we came. The porter had assisted me to carry my invalid downstairs, in a carrying-chair hired (like the landau) from Harrod's Stores for the occasion.

It was little after nine when we crawled together into the gardens; by half-past my invalid had had enough, and out he tottered on my arm; a cab, a message to our coachman, a timely train to Baker Street, another cab, and we were at the British Museum—brisk pedestrians now—not very many minutes after the opening hour of 10 A.M.

It was one of those glowing days which will not be forgotten by many who were in town at the time. The Diamond Jubilee was upon us, and Queen's weather had already set in. Raffles, indeed, declared it was as hot as Italy and Australia put together; and certainly the short summer nights gave the channels of wood and asphalt and the continents of brick and mortar but little time to cool. At the British Museum the pigeons were crooning among the shadows of the grimy colonnade, and the stalwart janitors looked less stalwart than usual, as though their medals were too heavy for them. I recognized some habitual Readers going to their labor underneath the dome; of mere visitors we seemed among the first.

"That's the room," said Raffles, who had bought the two-penny guide, as we studied it openly on the nearest bench; "number 43, upstairs and sharp round to the right. Come on, Bunny!"

And he led the way in silence, but with a long methodical stride which I could not understand until we came to the corridor leading to the Room of Gold, when he turned to me for a moment.

"A hundred and thirty-nine yards from this to the open street," said

Raffles, "not counting the stairs. I suppose we COULD do it in twenty seconds, but if we did we should have to jump the gates. No, you must remember to loaf out at slow march, Bunny, whether you like it or not."

"But you talked about a hiding-place for a night?"

"Quite so—for all night. We should have to get back, go on lying low, and saunter out with the crowd next day—after doing the whole show thoroughly."

"What! With gold in our pockets—"

"And gold in our boots, and gold up the sleeves and legs of our suits! You leave that to me, Bunny, and wait till you've tried two pairs of trousers sewn together at the foot! This is only a preliminary reconnoitre. And here we are."

It is none of my business to describe the so-called Room of Gold, with which I, for one, was not a little disappointed. The glass cases, which both fill and line it, may contain unique examples of the goldsmith's art in times and places of which one heard quite enough in the course of one's classical education; but, from a professional point of view, I would as lief have the ransacking of a single window in the West End as the pick of all those spoils of Etruria and of ancient Greece. The gold may not be so soft as it appears, but it certainly looks as though you could bite off the business ends of the spoons, and stop your own teeth in doing so. Nor should I care to be seen wearing one of the rings; but the greatest fraud of all (from the aforesaid standpoint) is assuredly that very cup of which Raffles had spoken. Moreover, he felt this himself.

"Why, it's as thin as paper," said he, "and enamelled like a middle-aged lady of quality! But, by Jove, it's one of the most beautiful things I ever saw in my life, Bunny. I should like to have it for its own sake, by all my gods!"

The thing had a little square case of plate-glass all to itself at one end of the room. It may have been the thing of beauty that Raffles affected to consider it, but I for my part was in no mood to look at it in that light. Underneath were the names of the plutocrats who had subscribed for this national gewgaw, and I fell to wondering where their £8,000 came in, while Raffles devoured his two-penny guide-book as greedily as a school-girl with a zeal for culture.

"Those are scenes from the martyrdom of St. Agnes," said he. . . "'translucent on relief. . . one of the finest specimens of its kind.' I should think it was! Bunny, you Philistine, why can't you admire the thing for its own sake? It would be worth having only to live up to! There never was such rich enamelling on such thin gold; and what a good scheme to hang the lid up over it, so that you can see how thin it is. I wonder if we could lift it, Bunny, by hook or crook?"

"You'd better try, sir," said a dry voice at his elbow.

The madman seemed to think we had the room to ourselves. I knew better, but, like another madman, had let him ramble on unchecked. And here was a stolid constable confronting us, in the short tunic that they wear in summer, his whistle on its chain, but no truncheon at his side. Heavens! how I see him now: a man of medium size, with a broad, good-humored, perspiring face, and a limp moustache. He looked sternly at Raffles, and Raffles looked merrily at him.

"Going to run me in, officer?" said he. "That WOULD be a joke—my hat!"

"I didn't say as I was, sir," replied the policeman. "But that's queer talk for a gentleman like you, sir, in the British Museum!" And he wagged his helmet at my invalid, who had taken his airing in frock-coat and top-hat, the more readily to assume his present part.

"What!" cried Raffles, "simply saying to my friend that I'd like to lift the gold cup? Why, so I should, officer, so I should! I don't mind who hears me say so. It's one of the most beautiful things I ever saw in all my life."

The constable's face had already relaxed, and now a grin peeped under the limp moustache. "I daresay there's many as feels like that, sir," said he.

"Exactly; and I say what I feel, that's all," said Raffles airily. "But seriously, officer, is a valuable thing like this quite safe in a case like that?"

"Safe enough as long as I'm here," replied the other, between grim jest and stout earnest. Raffles studied his face; he was still watching Raffles; and I kept an eye on them both without putting in my word.

"You appear to be single-handed," observed Raffles. "Is that wise?"

The note of anxiety was capitally caught; it was at once personal and public-spirited, that of the enthusiastic savant, afraid for a national treasure which few appreciated as he did himself. And, to be sure, the three of us now had this treasury to ourselves; one or two others had been there when we entered; but now they were gone.

"I'm not single-handed," said the officer, comfortably. "See that seat by the door? One of the attendants sits there all day long."

"Then where is he now?"

"Talking to another attendant just outside. If you listen you'll hear them for yourself."

We listened, and we did hear them, but not just outside. In my own mind I even questioned whether they were in the corridor through which we had come; to me it sounded as though they were just outside the corridor.

"You mean the fellow with the billiard-cue who was here when we came in?" pursued Raffles.

"That wasn't a billiard-cue! It was a pointer," the intelligent officer explained.

"It ought to be a javelin," said Raffles, nervously. "It ought to be a poleaxe! The public treasure ought to be better guarded than this. I shall write to the Times about it—you see if I don't!"

All at once, yet somehow not so suddenly as to excite suspicion, Raffles had become the elderly busybody with nerves; why, I could not for the life of me imagine; and the policeman seemed equally at sea.

"Lor' bless you, sir," said he, "I'm all right; don't you bother your head about ME."

"But you haven't even got a truncheon!"

"Not likely to want one either. You see, sir, it's early as yet; in a few minutes these here rooms will fill up; and there's safety in numbers, as they say."

"Oh, it will fill up soon, will it?"

"Any minute now, sir."

"Ah!"

"It isn't often empty as long as this, sir. It's the Jubilee, I suppose."

"Meanwhile, what if my friend and I had been professional thieves? Why, we could have over-powered you in an instant, my good fellow!"

"That you couldn't; leastways, not without bringing the whole place about your ears."

"Well, I shall write to the Times, all the same. I'm a connoisseur in all this sort of thing, and I won't have unnecessary risks run with the nation's property. You said there was an attendant just outside, but he sounds to me as though he were at the other end of the corridor. I shall write to-day!"

For an instant we all three listened; and Raffles was right. Then I saw two things in one glance. Raffles had stepped a few inches backward, and stood poised upon the ball of each foot, his arms half raised, a light in his eyes. And another kind of light was breaking over the crass features of our friend the constable.

"Then shall I tell you what I'LL do?" he cried, with a sudden clutch at the whistle-chain on his chest. The whistle flew out, but it never reached his lips. There were a couple of sharp smacks, like double barrels discharged all but simultaneously, and the man reeled against me so that I could not help catching him as he fell.

"Well done, Bunny! I've knocked him out—I've knocked him out! Run you to the door and see if the attendants have heard anything, and take them on if they have."

Mechanically I did as I was told. There was no time for thought, still less for remonstrance or reproach, though my surprise must have been even more complete than that of the constable before Raffles knocked the sense out of him. Even in my utter bewilderment, however, the instinctive caution of the real criminal did not desert me. I ran to the door, but I sauntered through it, to plant myself before a Pompeiian fresco in the corridor; and there were the two attendants still gossiping outside the further door; nor did they hear the dull crash which I heard even as I watched them out of the corner of each eye.

It was hot weather, as I have said, but the perspiration on my body seemed already to have turned into a skin of ice. Then I caught the faint reflection of my own face in the casing of the fresco, and it frightened me into some semblance of myself as Raffles joined me with his hands in his pockets. But my fear and indignation were redoubled at the sight of him, when a single glance convinced me that his pockets were as empty as his hands, and his mad outrage the most wanton and reckless of his whole career.

"Ah, very interesting, very interesting, but nothing to what they have in the museum at Naples or in Pompeii itself. You must go there some day, Bunny. I've a good mind to take you myself. Meanwhile—slow march! The beggar hasn't moved an eyelid. We may swing for him if you show indecent haste!"

"We!" I whispered. "We!"

And my knees knocked together as we came up to the chatting attendants. But Raffles must needs interrupt them to ask the way to the Prehistoric Saloon.

"At the top of the stairs."

"Thank you. Then we'll work round that way to the Egyptian part."

And we left them resuming their providential chat.

"I believe you're mad," I said bitterly as we went.

"I believe I was," admitted Raffles; "but I'm not now, and I'll see you through. A hundred and thirty-nine yards, wasn't it? Then it can't be more than a hundred and twenty now—not as much. Steady, Bunny, for God's sake. It's Slow march—for our lives."

There was this much management. The rest was our colossal luck. A hansom was being paid off at the foot of the steps outside, and in we jumped, Raffles shouting "Charing Cross!" for all Bloomsbury to hear.

We had turned into Bloomsbury Street without exchanging a syllable when he struck the trap-door with his fist.

"Where the devil are you driving us?"

"Charing Cross, sir."

"I said King's Cross! Round you spin, and drive like blazes, or we miss our train! There's one to York at 10:35," added Raffles as the trap-door slammed; "we'll book there, Bunny, and then we'll slope through the subway to the Metropolitan, and so to ground via Baker Street and Earl's Court."

And actually in half an hour he was seated once more in the hired carrying chair, while the porter and I staggered upstairs with my decrepit charge, for whose shattered strength even one hour in Kew Gardens had proved too much! Then, and not until then, when we had got rid of the porter and were alone at last, did I tell Raffles, in the most nervous English at my command, frankly and exactly what I thought of him and of his latest deed. Once started, moreover, I spoke as I have seldom spoken to living man; and Raffles, of all men, stood my abuse without a murmur; or rather he sat it out, too astounded even to take off his hat, though I thought his eyebrows would have lifted it from his head.

"But it always was your infernal way," I was savagely concluding. "You make one plan, and yet you tell me another—"

"Not to-day, Bunny, I swear!"

"You mean to tell me you really did start with the bare idea of finding a place to hide in for a night?"

"Of course I did."

"It was to be the mere reconnoitre you pretended?"

"There was no pretence about it, Bunny."

"Then why on earth go and do what you did?"

"The reason would be obvious to anyone but you," said Raffles, still with no unkindly scorn. "It was the temptation of a minute—the final impulse of the fraction of a second, when Roberto saw that I was tempted, and let me see that he saw it. It's not a thing I care to do, and I sha'n't be happy till the papers tell me the poor devil is alive. But a knock-out shot was the only chance for us then."

"Why? You don't get run in for being tempted, nor yet for showing that you are!"

"But I should have deserved running in if I hadn't yielded to such a temptation as that, Bunny. It was a chance in a hundred thousand! We might go there every day of our lives, and never again be the only outsiders in the room, with the billiard-marking Johnnie practically out of ear-shot at one and the same time. It was a gift from the gods; not to have taken it would have been flying in the face of Providence."

"But you didn't take it," said I. "You went and left it behind."

I wish I had had a Kodak for the little smile with which Raffles shook his head, for it was one that he kept for those great moments of which our vocation is not devoid. All this time he had been wearing his hat, tilted a little over eyebrows no longer raised. And now at last I knew where the gold cup was.

It stood for days upon his chimney-piece, this costly trophy whose ancient history and final fate filled newspaper columns even in these days of Jubilee, and for which the flower of Scotland Yard was said to be seeking high and low. Our constable, we learnt, had been stunned only, and, from the moment that I brought him an evening paper with the news, Raffles's spirits rose to a height inconsistent with his equable temperament, and as unusual in him as the sudden impulse upon which he had acted with such effect. The cup itself appealed to me no more than it had done before. Exquisite it might be, handsome it was, but so light in the hand that the mere gold of it would scarcely have poured three figures out of melting-pot. And what said Raffles but that he would never melt it at all!

"Taking it was an offence against the laws of the land, Bunny. That is nothing. But destroying it would be a crime against God and Art, and may I be spitted on the vane of St. Mary Abbot's if I commit it!"

Talk such as this was unanswerable; indeed, the whole affair had passed the pale of useful comment; and the one course left to a practical person was to shrug his shoulders and enjoy the joke. This was not a little enhanced by the newspaper reports, which described Raffles as a handsome youth, and his unwilling accomplice as an older man of blackguardly appearance and low type.

"Hits us both off rather neatly, Bunny," said he. "But what none of them do justice to is my dear cup. Look at it; only look at it, man! Was ever anything so rich and yet so chaste? St. Agnes must have had a pretty bad time, but it would be almost worth it to go down to posterity in such enamel upon such gold. And then the history of the thing. Do you realize that it's five hundred years old and has belonged to Henry the Eighth and to Elizabeth among others? Bunny, when you have me cremated, you can put my ashes in yonder cup, and lay us in the deep-delved earth together!"

"And meanwhile?"

"It is the joy of my heart, the light of my life, the delight of mine eye."

"And suppose other eyes catch sight of it?"

"They never must; they never shall."

Raffles would have been too absurd had he not been thoroughly alive to his own absurdity; there was nevertheless an underlying sincerity in his appreciation of any and every form of beauty, which all his nonsense could not conceal. And his infatuation for the cup was, as he declared, a very pure passion, since the circumstances debarred him from the chief joy of the average collector, that of showing his treasure to his friends. At last, however, and at the height of his craze, Raffles and reason seemed to come together again as suddenly as they had parted company in the Room of Gold.

"Bunny," he cried, flinging his newspaper across the room, "I've got an idea after your own heart. I know where I can place it after all!"

"Do you mean the cup?"

"I do."

"Then I congratulate you."

"Thanks."

"Upon the recovery of your senses."

"Thanks galore. But you've been confoundedly unsympathetic about this thing, Bunny, and I don't think I shall tell you my scheme till I've carried it out."

"Quite time enough," said I.

"It will mean your letting me loose for an hour or two under cloud of this very night. To-morrow's Sunday, the Jubilee's on Tuesday, and old Theobald's coming back for it."

"It doesn't much matter whether he's back or not if you go late enough."

"I mustn't be late. They don't keep open. No, it's no use your asking any questions. Go out and buy me a big box of Huntley & Palmer's biscuits; any sort you like, only they must be theirs, and absolutely the biggest box they sell."

"My dear man!"

"No questions, Bunny; you do your part and I'll do mine."

Subtlety and success were in his face. It was enough for me, and I had done his extraordinary bidding within a quarter of an hour. In another minute Raffles had opened the box and tumbled all the biscuits into the nearest chair.

"Now newspapers!"

I fetched a pile. He bid the cup of gold a ridiculous farewell, wrapped it up in newspaper after newspaper, and finally packed it in the empty biscuit-box.

"Now some brown paper. I don't want to be taken for the grocer's young man."

A neat enough parcel it made, when the string had been tied and the ends cut close; what was more difficult was to wrap up Raffles himself in such a way that even the porter should not recognize him if they came face to face at the corner. And the sun was still up. But Raffles would go, and when he did I should not have known him myself.

He may have been an hour away. It was barely dusk when he returned, and my first question referred to our dangerous ally, the porter. Raffles had passed him unsuspected in going, but had managed to avoid him altogether on the return journey, which he had completed by way of the other entrance and the roof. I breathed again.

"And what have you done with the cup?"

"Placed it!"

"How much for? How much for?"

"Let me think. I had a couple of cabs, and the postage was a tanner, with another twopence for registration. Yes, it cost me exactly five-and-eight."

"It cost You! But what did you Get for it, Raffles?"

"Nothing, my boy."

"Nothing!"

"Not a crimson cent."

"I am not surprised. I never thought it had a market value. I told you so in the beginning," I said, irritably. "But what on earth have you done with the thing?"

"Sent it to the Queen."

"You haven't!"

Rogue is a word with various meanings, and Raffles had been one sort of rogue ever since I had known him; but now, for once, he was the innocent variety, a great gray-haired child, running over with merriment and mischief.

"Well, I've sent it to Sir Arthur Bigge, to present to her Majesty, with the loyal respects of the thief, if that will do for you," said Raffles. "I thought they might take too much stock of me at the G.P.O. if I addressed it to the Sovereign her-self. Yes, I drove over to St. Martin's-le-Grand with it, and I registered the box into the bargain. Do a thing properly if you do it at all."

"But why on earth," I groaned, "do such a thing at all?"

"My dear Bunny, we have been reigned over for sixty years by infinitely the finest monarch the world has ever seen. The world is taking the present opportunity of signifying the fact for all it is worth. Every nation is laying of its best at her royal feet; every class in the community is doing its little level—except ours. All I have done is to remove one reproach from our fraternity."

At this I came round, was infected with his spirit, called him the sportsman he always was and would be, and shook his daredevil hand in mine; but, at the same time, I still had my qualms.

"Supposing they trace it to us?" said I.

"There's not much to catch hold of in a biscuit-box by Huntley & Palmer," replied Raffles; "that was why I sent you for one. And I didn't write a word upon a sheet of paper which could possibly be traced. I simply printed two or three on a virginal post-card—another half-penny to the bad—which might have been bought at any post-office in the kingdom. No, old chap, the G.P.O. was the one real danger; there was one detective I spotted for myself; and the sight of him has left me with a thirst. Whisky and Sullivans for two, Bunny, if you please."

Raffles was soon clinking his glass against mine.

"The Queen," said he. "God bless her!"

The Fate of Faustina

"Mar—ga—ri,
e perzo a Salvatore! Mar—ga—ri,
Ma l'ommo e cacciatore! Mar—ga—ri,
Nun ce aje corpa tu!
Chello ch' e fatto, e fatto, un ne parlammo cchieu!"

A piano-organ was pouring the metallic music through our open windows, while a voice of brass brayed the words, which I have since obtained, and print above for identification by such as know their Italy better than I. They will not thank me for reminding them of a tune so lately epidemic in that land of aloes and blue skies; but at least it is unlikely to run in their heads as the ribald accompaniment to a tragedy; and it does in mine.

It was in the early heat of August, and the hour that of the lawful and necessary siesta for such as turn night into day. I was therefore shutting my window in a rage, and wondering whether I should not do the same for Raffles, when he appeared in the silk pajamas to which the chronic solicitude of Dr. Theobald confined him from morning to night.

"Don't do that, Bunny," said he. "I rather like that thing, and want to listen. What sort of fellows are they to look at, by the way?"

I put my head out to see, it being a primary rule of our quaint establishment that Raffles must never show himself at any of the windows. I remember now how hot the sill was to my elbows, as I leant upon it and looked down, in order to satisfy a curiosity in which I could see no point.

"Dirty-looking beggars," said I over my shoulder: "dark as dark; blue chins, oleaginous curls, and ear-rings; ragged as they make them, but nothing picturesque in their rags."

"Neapolitans all over," murmured Raffles behind me; "and that's a characteristic touch, the one fellow singing while the other grinds; they always have that out there."

"He's rather a fine chap, the singer," said I, as the song ended. "My hat, what teeth! He's looking up here, and grinning all round his head; shall I chuck him anything?"

"Well, I have no reason to love the Neapolitans; but it takes me back—it takes me back! Yes, here you are, one each."

E.W. HORNUNG

It was a couple of half-crowns that Raffles put into my hand, but I had thrown them into the street for pennies before I saw what they were. Thereupon I left the Italians bowing to the mud, as well they might, and I turned to protest against such wanton waste. But Raffles was walking up and down, his head bent, his eyes troubled; and his one excuse disarmed remonstrance.

"They took me back," he repeated. "My God, how they took me back!"

Suddenly he stopped in his stride.

"You don't understand, Bunny, old chap; but if you like you shall. I always meant to tell you some day, but never felt worked up to it before, and it's not the kind of thing one talks about for talking's sake. It isn't a nursery story, Bunny, and there isn't a laugh in it from start to finish; on the contrary, you have often asked me what turned my hair gray, and now you are going to hear."

This was promising, but Raffles's manner was something more. It was unique in my memory of the man. His fine face softened and set hard by turns. I never knew it so hard. I never knew it so soft. And the same might be said of his voice, now tender as any woman's, now flying to the other extreme of equally unwonted ferocity. But this was toward the end of his tale; the beginning he treated characteristically enough, though I could have wished for a less cavalier account of the island of Elba, where, upon his own showing, he had met with much humanity.

"Deadly, my dear Bunny, is not the word for that glorified snag, or for the mollusks, its inhabitants. But they started by wounding my vanity, so perhaps I am prejudiced, after all. I sprung myself upon them as a shipwrecked sailor—a sole survivor—stripped in the sea and landed without a stitch—yet they took no more interest in me than you do in Italian organ-grinders. They were decent enough. I didn't have to pick and steal for a square meal and a pair of trousers; it would have been more exciting if I had. But what a place! Napoleon couldn't stand it, you remember, but he held on longer than I did. I put in a few weeks in their infernal mines, simply to pick up a smattering of Italian; then got across to the mainland in a little wooden timber-tramp; and ungratefully glad I was to leave Elba blazing in just such another sunset as the one you won't forget.

"The tramp was bound for Naples, but first it touched at Baiae, where I carefully deserted in the night. There are too many English in Naples itself, though I thought it would make a first happy hunting-ground when I knew the language better and had altered myself a bit more. Meanwhile I got a billet of several sorts on one of the loveliest spots that ever I struck on all my travels. The place was a vineyard, but it overhung the sea, and I got taken on as tame sailorman and emergency bottle-washer. The wages were the noble figure of a lira and a half, which is just over a bob, a day, but there were lashings of sound wine for one and all, and better wine to bathe in. And for eight whole months, my boy, I was an absolutely honest man. The luxury of it, Bunny! I out-heroded Herod, wouldn't touch a grape, and went in the most delicious danger of being knifed for my principles by the thieving crew I had joined.

"It was the kind of place where every prospect pleases—and all the rest of it—especially all the rest. But may I see it in my dreams till I die—as it was in the beginning—before anything began to happen. It was a wedge of rock sticking out into the bay, thatched with vines, and with the rummiest old house on the very edge of all, a devil of a height above the sea: you might have sat at the windows and dropped your Sullivan-ends plumb into blue water a hundred and fifty feet below.

"From the garden behind the house—such a garden, Bunny—oleanders and mimosa, myrtles, rosemarys and red tangles of fiery, untamed flowers—in a corner of this garden was the top of a subterranean stair down to the sea; at least there were nearly two hundred steps tunnelled through the solid rock; then an iron gate, and another eighty steps in the open air; and last of all a cave fit for pirates, a-penny-plain-and-two-pence-colored. This cave gave upon the sweetest little thing in coves, all deep blue water and honest rocks; and here I looked after the vineyard shipping, a pot-bellied tub with a brown sail, and a sort of dingy. The tub took the wine to Naples, and the dingy was the tub's tender.

"The house above was said to be on the identical site of a suburban retreat of the admirable Tiberius; there was the old sinner's private theatre with the tiers cut clean to this day, the well where he used to fatten his lampreys on his slaves, and a ruined temple of those ripping old Roman bricks, shallow as dominoes and ruddier than the cherry. I never was much of an antiquary, but I could have become one there if I'd had nothing else to do; but I had lots. When I wasn't busy with the boats I had to trim the vines, or gather the grapes, or even help make the wine itself in a cool, dark, musty vault underneath the temple, that I can see and smell as I jaw. And can't I hear it and feel it too! Squish, squash, bubble; squash, squish, guggle; and your feet as though you had

E.W. HORNUNG

been wading through slaughter to a throne. Yes, Bunny, you mightn't think it, but this good right foot, that never was on the wrong side of the crease when the ball left my hand, has also been known to

> 'crush the lees of pleasure
> From sanguine grapes of pain.'"

He made a sudden pause, as though he had stumbled on the truth in jest. His face filled with lines. We were sitting in the room that had been bare when first I saw it; there were basket-chairs and a table in it now, all meant ostensibly for me; and hence Raffles would slip to his bed, with schoolboy relish, at every tinkle of the bell. This afternoon we felt fairly safe, for Theobald had called in the morning, and Mrs. Theobald still took up much of his time. Through the open window we could hear the piano-organ and "Mar—gar—ri" a few hundred yards further on. I fancied Raffles was listening to it while he paused. He shook his head abstractedly when I handed him the cigarettes; and his tone hereafter was never just what it had been.

"I don't know, Bunny, whether you're a believer in transmigration of souls. I have often thought it easier to believe than lots of other things, and I have been pretty near believing in it myself since I had my being on that villa of Tiberius. The brute who had it in my day, if he isn't still running it with a whole skin, was or is as cold-blooded a blackguard as the worst of the emperors, but I have often thought he had a lot in common with Tiberius. He had the great high sensual Roman nose, eyes that were sinks of iniquity in themselves, and that swelled with fatness, like the rest of him, so that he wheezed if he walked a yard; otherwise rather a fine beast to look at, with a huge gray moustache, like a flying gull, and the most courteous manners even to his men; but one of the worst, Bunny, one of the worst that ever was. It was said that the vineyard was only his hobby; if so, he did his best to make his hobby pay. He used to come out from Naples for the week-ends—in the tub when it wasn't too rough for his nerves—and he didn't always come alone. His very name sounded unhealthy—Corbucci. I suppose I ought to add that he was a Count, though Counts are two-a-penny in Naples, and in season all the year round.

"He had a little English, and liked to air it upon me, much to my disgust; if I could not hope to conceal my nationality as yet, I at least did not want to have it advertised; and the swine had English friends.

When he heard that I was bathing in November, when the bay is still as warm as new milk, he would shake his wicked old head and say, 'You are very audashuss—you are very audashuss!' and put on no end of side before his Italians. By God, he had pitched upon the right word unawares, and I let him know it in the end!

"But that bathing, Bunny; it was absolutely the best I ever had anywhere. I said just now the water was like wine; in my own mind I used to call it blue champagne, and was rather annoyed that I had no one to admire the phrase. Otherwise I assure you that I missed my own particular kind very little indeed, though I often wished that YOU were there, old chap; particularly when I went for my lonesome swim; first thing in the morning, when the Bay was all rose-leaves, and last thing at night, when your body caught phosphorescent fire! Ah, yes, it was a good enough life for a change; a perfect paradise to lie low in; another Eden until. . .

"My poor Eve!"

And he fetched a sigh that took away his words; then his jaws snapped together, and his eyes spoke terribly while he conquered his emotion. I pen the last word advisedly. I fancy it is one which I have never used before in writing of A. J. Raffles, for I cannot at the moment recall any other occasion upon which its use would have been justified. On resuming, however, he was not only calm, but cold; and this flying for safety to the other extreme is the single instance of self-distrust which the present Achates can record to the credit of his impious Æneas.

"I called the girl Eve," said he. "Her real name was Faustina, and she was one of a vast family who hung out in a hovel on the inland border of the vineyard. And Aphrodite rising from the sea was less wonderful and not more beautiful than Aphrodite emerging from that hole!

"It was the most exquisite face I ever saw or shall see in this life. Absolutely perfect features; a skin that reminded you of old gold, so delicate was its bronze; magnificent hair, not black but nearly; and such eyes and teeth as would have made the fortune of a face without another point. I tell you, Bunny, London would go mad about a girl like that. But I don't believe there's such another in the world. And there she was wasting her sweetness upon that lovely but desolate little corner of it! Well, she did not waste it upon me. I would have married her, and lived happily ever after in such a hovel as her people's—with her. Only to look at her—only to look at her for the rest of my days—I could have lain low and remained dead even to you! And that's all I'm going to tell you about that, Bunny; cursed be he who tells more! Yet don't run away with the idea that this poor Faustina was the only woman I ever cared about. I don't believe in all that 'only' rot; nevertheless I tell you that she was the one being who ever entirely satisfied my sense of beauty; and I honestly believe I could have chucked the world and been true to Faustina for that alone.

"We met sometimes in the little temple I told you about, sometimes among the vines; now by honest accident, now by flagrant design; and found a ready-made rendezvous, romantic as one could wish, in the cave down all those subterranean steps. Then the sea would call us—my blue champagne—my sparkling cobalt—and there was the dingy ready to our hand. Oh, those nights! I never knew which I liked best, the moonlit ones when you sculled through silver and could see for miles, or the dark nights when the fishermen's torches stood for the sea, and a red zig-zag in the sky for old Vesuvius. We were happy. I don't mind owning it. We seemed not to have a care between us. My mates took no interest in my affairs, and Faustina's family did not appear to bother about her. The Count was in Naples five nights of the seven; the other two we sighed apart.

"At first it was the oldest story in literature—Eden plus Eve. The place had been a heaven on earth before, but now it was heaven itself. So for a little; then one night, a Monday night, Faustina burst out crying in the boat; and sobbed her story as we drifted without mishap by the mercy of the Lord. And that was almost as old a story as the other.

"She was engaged—what! Had I never heard of it? Did I mean to upset the boat? What was her engagement beside our love? 'Niente, niente,' crooned Faustina, sighing yet smiling through her tears. No, but what did matter was that the man had threatened to stab her to the heart—and would do it as soon as look at her—that I knew.

"I knew it merely from my knowledge of the Neapolitans, for I had no idea who the man might be. I knew it, and yet I took this detail better than the fact of the engagement, though now I began to laugh at both. As if I was going to let her marry anybody else! As if a hair of her lovely head should be touched while I lived to protect her! I had a great mind to row away to blazes with her that very night, and never go near the vineyard again, or let her either. But we had not a lira between us at the time, and only the rags in which we sat barefoot in the boat. Besides, I had to know the name of the animal who had threatened a woman, and such a woman as this.

"For a long time she refused to tell me, with splendid obduracy; but I was as determined as she; so at last she made conditions. I was not to go and get put in prison for sticking a knife into him—he wasn't worth it—and I did promise not to stab him in the back. Faustina seemed quite satisfied, though a little puzzled by my manner, having herself the racial tolerance for cold steel; and next moment she had taken away my breath. 'It is Stefano,' she whispered, and hung her head.

"And well she might, poor thing! Stefano, of all creatures on God's earth—for her!

"Bunny, he was a miserable little undersized wretch—ill-favored—servile—surly—and second only to his master in bestial cunning and hypocrisy. His face was enough for me; that was what I read in it, and I don't often make mistakes. He was Corbucci's own confidential body-servant, and that alone was enough to damn him in decent eyes: always came out first on the Saturday with the spese, to have all ready for his master and current mistress, and stayed behind on the Monday to clear and lock up. Stefano! That worm! I could well understand his threatening a woman with a knife; what beat me was how any woman could ever have listened to him; above all, that Faustina should be the one! It passed my comprehension. But I questioned her as gently as I could; and her explanation was largely the thread-bare one you would expect. Her parents were so poor. They were so many in family. Some of them begged—would I promise never to tell? Then some of them stole—sometimes—and all knew the pains of actual want. She looked after the cows, but there were only two of them, and brought the milk to the vineyard and elsewhere; but that was not employment for more than one; and there were countless sisters waiting to take her place. Then he was so rich, Stefano.

"'Rich!' I echoed. 'Stefano?'

"'Si, Arturo mio.'

"Yes, I played the game on that vineyard, Bunny, even to going my own first name.

"'And how comes he to be rich?' I asked, suspiciously.

"She did not know; but he had given her such beautiful jewels; the family had lived on them for months, she pretending an avocat had taken charge of them for her against her marriage. But I cared nothing about all that.

"'Jewels! Stefano!' I could only mutter.

"'Perhaps the Count has paid for some of them. He is very kind.'

"'To you, is he?'

"'Oh, yes, very kind.'

"'And you would live in his house afterwards?'

"'Not now, mia cara—not now!'

"'No, by God you don't!' said I in English. 'But you would have done so, eh?'

"'Of course. That was arranged. The Count is really very kind.'

"'Do you see anything of him when he comes here?'

"Yes, he had sometimes brought her little presents, sweetmeats, ribbons, and the like; but the offering had always been made through this toad of a Stefano. Knowing the men, I now knew all. But Faustina, she had the pure and simple heart, and the white soul, by the God who made it, and for all her kindness to a tattered scapegrace who made love to her in broken Italian between the ripples and the stars. She was not to know what I was, remember; and beside Corbucci and his henchman I was the Archangel Gabriel come down to earth.

"Well, as I lay awake that night, two more lines of Swinburne came into my head, and came to stay:

"God said 'Let him who wins her take
And keep Faustine.'

"On that couplet I slept at last, and it was my text and watchword when I awoke in the morning. I forget how well you know your Swinburne, Bunny; but don't you run away with the idea that there was anything else in common between his Faustine and mine. For the last time let me tell you that poor Faustina was the whitest and the best I ever knew.

"Well, I was strung up for trouble when the next Saturday came, and I'll tell you what I had done. I had broken the pledge and burgled Corbucci's villa in my best manner during his absence in Naples. Not that it gave me the slightest trouble; but no human being could have told that I had been in, when I came out. And I had stolen nothing, mark you, but only borrowed a revolver from a drawer in the Count's desk, with one or two trifling accessories; for by this time I had the measure of these damned Neapolitans. They are spry enough with a knife, but you show them the business end of a shooting-iron, and they'll streak like rabbits for the nearest hole. But the revolver wasn't for my own use. It was for Faustina, and I taught her how to use it in the cave down there by the sea, shooting at candles stuck upon the rock. The noise in the cave was something frightful, but high up above it couldn't be heard at all, as we proved to each other's satisfaction pretty early in the proceedings. So now Faustina was armed with munitions of self-defence; and I knew enough of her character to entertain no doubt as to their spirited use upon occasion. Between the two of us, in fact, our friend Stefano seemed tolerably certain of a warm week-end.

"But the Saturday brought word that the Count was not coming this week, being in Rome on business, and unable to return in time; so for a whole Sunday we were promised peace; and made bold plans accordingly. There was no further merit in hushing this thing up. 'Let him who wins her take and keep Faustine.' Yes, but let him win her openly, or lose her and be damned to him! So on the Sunday I was going to have it out with her people—with the Count and Stefano as soon as they showed their noses. I had no inducement, remember, ever to return to surreptitious life within a cab-fare of Wormwood Scrubbs. Faustina and the Bay of Naples were quite good enough for me. And the prehistoric man in me rather exulted in the idea of fighting for my desire.

"On the Saturday, however, we were able to meet for the last time as heretofore—just once more in secret—down there in the cave—as soon as might be after dark. Neither of us minded if we were kept for hours; each knew in the end that the other would come; and there was a charm of its own even in waiting with such knowledge. But that night I did lose patience: not in the cave, but up above, where first on one pretext and then on another the direttore kept me going until I smelt a rat. He was not given to exacting overtime, this direttore, whose only fault was his servile subjection to our common boss. It seemed pretty obvious, therefore, that he was acting upon some secret instructions from Corbucci himself, and, the moment I suspected this, I asked him to his face if it was not the case. And it was; he admitted it with many shrugs, being a conveniently weak person, whom one felt almost ashamed of bullying as the occasion demanded.

"The fact was, however, that the Count had sent for him on finding he had to go to Rome, and had said he was very sorry to go just then, as among other things he intended to speak to me about Faustina. Stefano had told him all about his row with her, and moreover that it was on my account, which Faustina had never told me, though I had guessed as much for myself. Well, the Count was going to take his jackal's part for all he was worth, which was just exactly what I had expected him to do. He intended going for me on his return, but meanwhile I was not to make hay in his absence, and so this tool of a direttore had orders to keep me at it night and day. I undertook not to give the poor beast away, but at the same time told him I had not the faintest intention of doing another stroke of work that night.

"It was very dark, and I remember knocking my head against the oranges as I ran up the long, shallow steps which ended the journey between the direttore's lodge and the villa itself. But at the back of the villa was the garden I spoke about, and also a bare chunk of the cliff where it was bored by that subterranean stair. So I saw the stars close overhead, and the fishermen's torches far below, the coastwise lights and the crimson hieroglyph that spelt Vesuvius, before I plunged into the darkness of the shaft. And that was the last time I appreciated the unique and peaceful charm of this outlandish spot.

"The stair was in two long flights, with an air-hole or two at the top of the upper one, but not another pin-prick till you came to the iron gate at the bottom of the lower. As you may read of an infinitely lighter place, in a finer work of fiction than you are ever likely to write, Bunny, it was 'gloomy at noon, dark as midnight at dusk, and black as the ninth plague of Egypt at midnight.' I won't swear to my quotation, but I will to those stairs. They were as black that night as the inside of the safest safe in the strongest strong-room in the Chancery Lane Deposit. Yet I had not got far down them with my bare feet before I heard somebody else coming up in boots. You may imagine what a turn that gave me! It could not be Faustina, who went barefoot three seasons of the four, and yet there was Faustina waiting for me down below. What a fright she must have had! And all at once my own blood ran cold: for the man sang like a kettle as he plodded up and up. It was, it must be, the short-winded Count himself, whom we all supposed to be in Rome!

"Higher he came and nearer, nearer, slowly yet hurriedly, now stopping to cough and gasp, now taking a few steps by elephantine assault. I should have enjoyed the situation if it had not been for poor Faustina in the cave; as it was I was filled with nameless fears. But I could not resist giving that grampus Corbucci one bad moment on account. A crazy hand-rail ran up one wall, so I carefully flattened myself against the other, and he passed within six inches of me, puffing and wheezing like a brass band. I let him go a few steps higher, and then I let him have it with both lungs.

"Buona sera, eccellenza, signori!' I roared after him. And a scream came down in answer—such a scream! A dozen different terrors were in it; and the wheezing had stopped, with the old scoundrel's heart.

"'Chi sta la?' he squeaked at last, gibbering and whimpering like a whipped monkey, so that I could not bear to miss his face, and got a match all ready to strike.

"'Arturo, signori.'

"He didn't repeat my name, nor did he damn me in heaps. He did nothing but wheeze for a good minute, and when he spoke it was with insinuating civility, in his best English.

"'Come nearer, Arturo. You are in the lower regions down there. I want to speak with you.'

"'No, thanks. I'm in a hurry,' I said, and dropped that match back into my pocket. He might be armed, and I was not.

"'So you are in a 'urry!' and he wheezed amusement. 'And you thought I was still in Rome, no doubt; and so I was until this afternoon, when I caught train at the eleventh moment, and then another train from Naples to Pozzuoli. I have been rowed here now by a fisherman of Pozzuoli. I had not time to stop anywhere in Naples, but only to drive from station to station. So I am without Stefano, Arturo, I am without Stefano.'

"His sly voice sounded preternaturally sly in the absolute darkness, but even through that impenetrable veil I knew it for a sham. I had laid hold of the hand-rail. It shook violently in my hand; he also was holding it where he stood. And these suppressed tremors, or rather their detection in this way, struck a strange chill to my heart, just as I was beginning to pluck it up.

"'It is lucky for Stefano,' said I, grim as death.

"'Ah, but you must not be too 'ard on 'im,' remonstrated the Count. 'You have stole his girl, he speak with me about it, and I wish to speak with you. It is very audashuss, Arturo, very audashuss! Perhaps you are even going to meet her now, eh?'"

I told him straight that I was.

"'Then there is no 'urry, for she is not there.'

"'You didn't see her in the cave?' I cried, too delighted at the thought to keep it to myself.

"'I had no such fortune,' the old devil said.

"'She is there, all the same.'

"'I only wish I 'ad known.'

"'And I've kept her long enough!'

"In fact I threw this over my shoulder as I turned and went running down.

"'I 'ope you will find her!' his malicious voice came croaking after me. 'I 'ope you will—I 'ope so.'

"And find her I did."

Raffles had been on his feet some time, unable to sit still or to stand, moving excitedly about the room. But now he stood still enough, his elbows on the cast-iron mantelpiece, his head between his hands.

"Dead?" I whispered.

And he nodded to the wall.

"There was not a sound in the cave. There was no answer to my voice. Then I went in, and my foot touched hers, and it was colder than the rock. . . Bunny, they had stabbed her to the heart. She had fought them, and they had stabbed her to the heart!"

"You say 'they,'" I said gently, as he stood in heavy silence, his back still turned. "I thought Stefano had been left behind?"

Raffles was round in a flash, his face white-hot, his eyes dancing death.

"He was in the cave!" he shouted. "I saw him—I spotted him—it was broad twilight after those stairs—and I went for him with my bare hands. Not fists, Bunny; not fists for a thing like that; I meant getting my fingers into his vile little heart and tearing it out by the roots. I was stark mad. But he had the revolver—hers. He blazed it at arm's length, and missed. And that steadied me. I had smashed his funny-bone against the rock before he could blaze again; the revolver fell with a rattle, but without going off; in an instant I had it tight, and the little swine at my mercy at last."

"You didn't show him any?"

"Mercy? With Faustina dead at my feet? I should have deserved none in the next world if I had shown him any in this! No, I just stood over him, with the revolver in both hands, feeling the chambers with my thumb; and as I stood he stabbed at me; but I stepped back to that one, and brought him down with a bullet in his guts.

"'And I can spare you two or three more,' I said, for my poor girl could not have fired a shot. 'Take that one to hell with you—and that—and that!'

"Then I started coughing and wheezing like the Count himself, for the place was full of smoke. When it cleared my man was very dead, and I tipped him into the sea, to defile that rather than Faustina's cave. And then—and then—we were alone for the last time, she and I, in our own pet haunt; and I could scarcely see her, yet I would not strike a match, for I knew she would not have me see her as she was. I could say good-by to her without that. I said it; and I left her like a man, and up the first open-air steps with my head in the air and the stars all sharp in the sky; then suddenly they swam, and back I went like a lunatic, to see if she was really dead, to bring her back to life. . . Bunny, I can't tell you any more."

"Not of the Count?" I murmured at last.

"Not even of the Count," said Raffles, turning round with a sigh. "I left him pretty sorry for himself; but what was the good of that? I had taken blood for blood, and it was not Corbucci who had killed Faustina. No, the plan was his, but that was not part of the plan. They had found out about our meetings in the cave: nothing simpler than to have me kept hard at it overhead and to carry off Faustina by brute force in the boat. It was their only chance, for she had said more to Stefano than she had admitted to me, and more than I am going to repeat about myself. No persuasion would have induced her to listen to him again; so they tried force; and she drew Corbucci's revolver on them, but they had taken her by surprise, and Stefano stabbed her before she could fire."

"But how do you know all that?" I asked Raffles, for his tale was going to pieces in the telling, and the tragic end of poor Faustina was no ending for me.

"Oh," said he, "I had it from Corbucci at his own revolver's point. He was waiting at his window, and I could have potted him at my ease where he stood against the light listening hard enough but not seeing a thing. So he asked whether it was Stefano, and I whispered, 'Si, signore'; and then whether he had finished Arturo, and I brought the same shot off again. He had let me in before he knew who was finished and who was not."

"And did you finish him?"

"No; that was too good for Corbucci. But I bound and gagged him about as tight as man was ever gagged or bound, and I left him in his room with the shutters shut and the house locked up. The shutters of that old place were six inches thick, and the walls nearly six feet; that was on the Saturday night, and the Count wasn't expected at the vineyard before the following Saturday. Meanwhile he was supposed to be in Rome. But the dead would doubtless be discovered next day, and I am afraid this would lead to his own discovery with the life still in him. I believe he figured on that himself, for he sat threatening me gamely till the last. You never saw such a sight as he was, with his head split in two by a ruler tied at the back of it, and his great moustache pushed up into his bulging eyes. But I locked him up in the dark without a qualm, and I wished and still wish him every torment of the damned."

"And then?"

"The night was still young, and within ten miles there was the best of ports in a storm, and hundreds of holds for the humble stowaway to choose from. But I didn't want to go further than Genoa, for by this time my Italian would wash, so I chose the old Norddeutscher Lloyd, and had an excellent voyage in one of the boats slung in-board over the bridge. That's better than any hold, Bunny, and I did splendidly on oranges brought from the vineyard."

"And at Genoa?"

"At Genoa I took to my wits once more, and have been living on nothing else ever since. But there I had to begin all over again, and at the very bottom of the ladder. I slept in the streets. I begged. I did all manner of terrible things, rather hoping for a bad end, but never coming to one. Then one day I saw a white-headed old chap looking at me through a shop-window—a window I had designs upon—and when I stared at him he stared at me—and we wore the same rags. So I had come to that! But one reflection makes many. I had not recognized myself; who on earth would recognize me? London called me—and here I am. Italy had broken my heart—and there it stays."

Flippant as a schoolboy one moment, playful even in the bitterness of the next, and now no longer giving way to the feeling which had spoilt the climax of his tale, Raffles needed knowing as I alone knew him for a right appreciation of those last words. That they were no mere words I know full well. That, but for the tragedy of his Italian life, that life would have sufficed him for years, if not for ever, I did and do still believe. But I alone see him as I saw him then, the lines upon his face, and the pain behind the lines; how they came to disappear, and what removed them, you will never guess. It was the one thing you would have expected to have the opposite effect, the thing indeed that had forced his confidence, the organ and the voice once more beneath our very windows:

> "Margarita de Parete,
> era a' sarta d' e' signore;
> se pugneva sempe e ddete
> pe penzare a Salvatore!

"Mar—ga—ri,
e perzo e Salvatore!
Mar—ga—ri,
Ma l'ommo e cacciatore!
Mar—ga—ri,
Nun ce aje corpa tu!
Chello ch' e fatto, e fatto, un ne parlammo cchieu!"

I simply stared at Raffles. Instead of deepening, his lines had vanished. He looked years younger, mischievous and merry and alert as I remembered him of old in the breathless crisis of some madcap escapade. He was holding up his finger; he was stealing to the window; he was peeping through the blind as though our side street were Scotland Yard itself; he was stealing back again, all revelry, excitement, and suspense.

"I half thought they were after me before," said he. "That was why I made you look. I daren't take a proper look myself, but what a jest if they were! What a jest!"

"Do you mean the police?" said I.

"The police! Bunny, do you know them and me so little that you can look me in the face and ask such a question? My boy, I'm dead to them—off their books—a good deal deader than being off the hooks! Why, if I went to Scotland Yard this minute, to give myself up, they'd chuck me out for a harmless lunatic. No, I fear an enemy nowadays, and I go in terror of the sometime friend, but I have the utmost confidence in the dear police."

"Then whom do you mean?"

"The Camorra!"

I repeated the word with a different intonation. Not that I had never heard of that most powerful and sinister of secret societies; but I failed to see on what grounds Raffles should jump to the conclusion that these everyday organ-grinders belonged to it.

"It was one of Corbucci's threats," said he. "If I killed him the Camorra would certainly kill me; he kept on telling me so; it was like his cunning not to say that he would put them on my tracks whether or no."

"He is probably a member himself!"

"Obviously, from what he said."

"But why on earth should you think that these fellows are?" I demanded, as that brazen voice came rasping through a second verse.

"I don't think. It was only an idea. That thing is so thoroughly Neapolitan, and I never heard it on a London organ before. Then again, what should bring them back here?"

I peeped through the blind in my turn; and, to be sure, there was the fellow with the blue chin and the white teeth watching our windows, and ours only, as he bawled.

"And why?" cried Raffles, his eyes dancing when I told him.

"Why should they come sneaking back to us? Doesn't that look suspicious, Bunny; doesn't that promise a lark?"

"Not to me," I said, having the smile for once. "How many people, should you imagine, toss them five shilling for as many minutes of their infernal row? You seem to forget that's what you did an hour ago!"

Raffles had forgotten. His blank face confessed the fact. Then suddenly he burst outlaughing at himself.

"Bunny," said he, "you've no imagination, and I never knew I had so much! Of course you're right. I only wish you were not, for there's nothing I should enjoy more than taking on another Neapolitan or two. You see, I owe them something still! I didn't settle in full. I owe them more than ever I shall pay them on this side Styx!"

He had hardened even as he spoke: the lines and the years had come again, and his eyes were flint and steel, with an honest grief behind the glitter.

The Last Laugh

As I have had occasion to remark elsewhere, the pick of our exploits, from a frankly criminal point of view, are of least use for the comparatively pure purposes of these papers. They might be appreciated in a trade journal (if only that want could be supplied), by skilled manipulators of the jemmy and the large light bunch; but, as records of unbroken yet insignificant success, they would be found at once too trivial and too technical, if not sordid and unprofitable into the bargain. The latter epithets, and worse, have indeed already been applied, if not to Raffles and all his works, at least to mine upon Raffles, by more than one worthy wielder of a virtuous pen. I need not say how heartily I disagree with that truly pious opinion. So far from admitting a single word of it, I maintain it is the liveliest warning that I am giving to the world. Raffles was a genius, and he could not make it pay! Raffles had invention, resource, incomparable audacity, and a nerve in ten thousand. He was both strategian and tactician, and we all now know the difference between the two. Yet for months he had been hiding like a rat in a hole, unable to show even his altered face by night or day without risk, unless another risk were courted by three inches of conspicuous crepe. Then thus far our rewards had oftener than not been no reward at all. Altogether it was a very different story from the old festive, unsuspected, club and cricket days, with their noctes ambrosianae at the Albany.

And now, in addition to the eternal peril of recognition, there was yet another menace of which I knew nothing. I thought no more of our Neapolitan organ-grinders, though I did often think of the moving page that they had torn for me out of my friend's strange life in Italy. Raffles never alluded to the subject again, and for my part I had entirely forgotten his wild ideas connecting the organ-grinders with the Camorra, and imagining them upon his own tracks. I heard no more of it, and thought as little, as I say. Then one night in the autumn—I shrink from shocking the susceptible for nothing—but there was a certain house in Palace Gardens, and when we got there Raffles would pass on. I could see no soul in sight, no glimmer in the windows. But Raffles had my arm, and on we went without talking about it. Sharp to the left on the Notting Hill side, sharper still up Silver Street, a little tacking west and south, a plunge across High Street, and presently we were home.

"Pyjamas first," said Raffles, with as much authority as though it mattered. It was a warm night, however, though September, and I did not mind until I came in clad as he commanded to find the autocrat himself still booted and capped. He was peeping through the blind, and the gas was still turned down. But he said that I could turn it up, as he helped himself to a cigarette and nothing with it.

"May I mix you one?" said I.

"No, thanks."

"What's the trouble?"

"We were followed."

"Never!"

"You never saw it."

"But You never looked round."

"I have an eye at the back of each ear, Bunny."

I helped myself and I fear with less moderation than might have been the case a minute before.

"So that was why—"

"That was why," said Raffles, nodding; but he did not smile, and I put down my glass untouched.

"They were following us then!"

"All up Palace Gardens."

"I thought you wound about coming back over the hill."

"Nevertheless, one of them's in the street below at this moment."

No, he was not fooling me. He was very grim. And he had not taken off a thing; perhaps he did not think it worth while.

"Plain clothes?" I sighed, following the sartorial train of thought, even to the loathly arrows that had decorated my person once already for a little aeon. Next time they would give me double. The skilly was in my stomach when I saw Raffles's face.

"Who said it was the police, Bunny?" said he. "It's the Italians. They're only after me; they won't hurt a hair of Your head, let alone cropping it! Have a drink, and don't mind me. I shall score them off before I'm done."

"And I'll help you!"

"No, old chap, you won't. This is my own little show. I've known about it for weeks. I first tumbled to it the day those Neapolitans came back with their organs, though I didn't seriously suspect things then; they never came again, those two, they had done their part. That's the Camorra all over, from all accounts. The Count I told you about is pretty high up in it, by the way he spoke, but there will be grades and grades between him and the organ-grinders. I shouldn't be surprised if he had every low-down Neapolitan ice-creamer in the town upon my tracks! The organization's incredible. Then do you remember the superior foreigner who came to the door a few days afterwards? You said he had velvet eyes."

"I never connected him with those two!"

"Of course you didn't, Bunny, so you threatened to kick the fellow downstairs, and only made them keener on the scent. It was too late to say anything when you told me. But the very next time I showed my nose outside I heard a camera click as I passed, and the fiend was a person with velvet eyes. Then there was a lull—that happened weeks ago. They had sent me to Italy for identification by Count Corbucci."

"But this is all theory," I exclaimed. "How on earth can you know?"

"I don't know," said Raffles, "but I should like to bet. Our friend the bloodhound is hanging about the corner near the pillar-box; look through my window, it's dark in there, and tell me who he is."

The man was too far away for me to swear to his face, but he wore a covert-coat of un-English length, and the lamp across the road played steadily on his boots; they were very yellow, and they made no noise when he took a turn. I strained my eyes, and all at once I remembered the thin-soled, low-heeled, splay yellow boots of the insidious foreigner, with the soft eyes and the brown-paper face, whom I had turned from the door as a palpable fraud. The ring at the bell was the first I had heard of him, there had been no warning step upon the stairs, and my suspicious eye had searched his feet for rubber soles.

"It's the fellow," I said, returning to Raffles, and I described his boots.

Raffles was delighted.

"Well done, Bunny; you're coming on," said he. "Now I wonder if he's been over here all the time, or if they sent him over expressly? You did better than you think in spotting those boots, for they can only have been made in Italy, and that looks like the special envoy. But it's no use speculating. I must find out."

"How can you?"

"He won't stay there all night."

"Well?"

"When he gets tired of it I shall return the compliment and follow Him."

"Not alone," said I, firmly.

"Well, we'll see. We'll see at once," said Raffles, rising. "Out with the gas, Bunny, while I take a look. Thank you. Now wait a bit. . . yes! He's chucked it; he's off already; and so am I!"

But I slipped to our outer door, and held the passage.

"I don't let you go alone, you know."

"You can't come with me in pyjamas."

"Now I see why you made me put them on!"

"Bunny, if you don't shift I shall have to shift you. This is my very own private one-man show. But I'll be back in an hour—there!"

"You swear?"

"By all my gods."

I gave in. How could I help giving in? He did not look the man that he had been, but you never knew with Raffles, and I could not have him lay a hand on me. I let him go with a shrug and my blessing, then ran into his room to see the last of him from the window.

The creature in the coat and boots had reached the end of our little street, where he appeared to have hesitated, so that Raffles was just in time to see which way he turned. And Raffles was after him at an easy pace, and had himself almost reached the corner when my attention was distracted from the alert nonchalance of his gait. I was marvelling that it alone had not long ago betrayed him, for nothing about him was so unconsciously characteristic, when suddenly I realized that Raffles was not the only person in the little lonely street. Another pedestrian had entered from the other end, a man heavily built and clad, with an astrakhan collar to his coat on this warm night, and a black slouch hat that hid his features from my bird's-eye view. His steps were the short and shuffling ones of a man advanced in years and in fatty degeneration, but of a sudden they stopped beneath my very eyes. I could have dropped a marble into the dinted crown of the black felt hat. Then, at the same moment, Raffles turned the corner without looking round, and the big man below raised both his hands and his face. Of the latter I saw only the huge white moustache, like a flying gull, as Raffles had described it; for at a glance I divined that this was his arch-enemy, the Count Corbucci himself.

I did not stop to consider the subtleties of the system by which the real hunter lagged behind while his subordinate pointed the quarry like a sporting dog. I left the Count shuffling onward faster than before, and I jumped into some clothes as though the flats were on fire. If the Count was going to follow Raffles in his turn, then I would follow the Count in mine, and there would be a midnight procession of us through the town. But I found no sign of him in the empty street, and no sign in the Earl's Court Road, that looked as empty for all its length, save for a natural enemy standing like a waxwork figure with a glimmer at his belt.

"Officer," I gasped, "have you seen anything of an old gentleman with a big white mustache?"

The unlicked cub of a common constable seemed to eye me the more suspiciously for the flattering form of my address.

"Took a hansom," said he at length.

A hansom! Then he was not following the others on foot; there was no guessing his game. But something must be said or done.

"He's a friend of mine," I explained, "and I want to overtake him. Did you hear where he told the fellow to drive?"

A curt negative was the policeman's reply to that; and if ever I take part in a night assault-at-arms, revolver versus baton, in the back kitchen, I know which member of the Metropolitan Police Force I should like for my opponent.

If there was no overtaking the Count, however, it should be a comparatively simple matter in the case of the couple on foot, and I wildly hailed the first hansom that crawled into my ken. I must tell Raffles who it was that I had seen; the Earl's Court Road was long, and the time since he vanished in it but a few short minutes. I drove down the length of that useful thoroughfare, with an eye apiece on either pavement, sweeping each as with a brush, but never a Raffles came into the pan. Then I tried the Fulham Road, first to the west, then to the east, and in the end drove home to the flat as bold as brass. I did not realize my indiscretion until I had paid the man and was on the stairs. Raffles never dreamt of driving all the way back; but I was hoping now to find him waiting up above. He had said an hour. I had remembered it suddenly. And now the hour was more than up. But the flat was as empty as I had left it; the very light that had encouraged me, pale though it was, as I turned the corner in my hansom, was but the light that I myself had left burning in the desolate passage.

I can give you no conception of the night that I spent. Most of it I hung across the sill, throwing a wide net with my ears, catching every footstep afar off, every hansom bell farther still, only to gather in some alien whom I seldom even landed in our street. Then I would listen at the door.

He might come over the roof; and eventually some one did; but now it was broad daylight, and I flung the door open in the milkman's face, which whitened at the shock as though I had ducked him in his own pail.

"You're late," I thundered as the first excuse for my excitement.

"Beg your pardon," said he, indignantly, "but I'm half an hour before my usual time."

"Then I beg yours," said I; "but the fact is, Mr. Maturin has had one of his bad nights, and I seem to have been waiting hours for milk to make him a cup of tea."

This little fib (ready enough for Raffles, though I say it) earned me not only forgiveness but that obliging sympathy which is a branch of the business of the man at the door. The good fellow said that he could see I had been sitting up all night, and he left me pluming myself upon the accidental art with which I had told my very necessary tarra-diddle. On reflection I gave the credit to instinct, not accident, and then sighed afresh as I realized how the influence of the master was sinking into me, and he Heaven knew where! But my punishment was swift to follow, for within the hour the bell rang imperiously twice, and there was Dr. Theobald on our mat; in a yellow Jaeger suit, with a chin as yellow jutting over the flaps that he had turned up to hide his pyjamas.

"What's this about a bad night?" said he.

"He couldn't sleep, and he wouldn't let me," I whispered, never loosening my grasp of the door, and standing tight against the other wall. "But he's sleeping like a baby now."

"I must see him."

"He gave strict orders that you should not."

"I'm his medical man, and I—"

"You know what he is," I said, shrugging; "the least thing wakes him, and you will if you insist on seeing him now. It will be the last time, I warn you! I know what he said, and you don't."

The doctor cursed me under his fiery moustache.

"I shall come up during the course of the morning," he snarled.

"And I shall tie up the bell," I said, "and if it doesn't ring he'll be sleeping still, but I will not risk waking him by coming to the door again."

And with that I shut it in his face. I was improving, as Raffles had said; but what would it profit me if some evil had befallen him? And now I was prepared for the worst. A boy came up whistling and leaving papers on the mats; it was getting on for eight o'clock, and the whiskey and soda of half-past twelve stood untouched and stagnant in the tumbler. If the worst had happened to Raffles, I felt that I would either never drink again, or else seldom do anything else.

Meanwhile I could not even break my fast, but roamed the flat in a misery not to be described, my very linen still unchanged, my cheeks and chin now tawny from the unwholesome night. How long would it go on? I wondered for a time. Then I changed my tune: how long could I endure it?

It went on actually until the forenoon only, but my endurance cannot be measured by the time, for to me every hour of it was an arctic night. Yet it cannot have been much after eleven when the ring came at the bell, which I had forgotten to tie up after all. But this was not the doctor; neither, too well I knew, was it the wanderer returned. Our bell was the pneumatic one that tells you if the touch be light or heavy; the hand upon it now was tentative and shy.

The owner of the hand I had never seen before. He was young and ragged, with one eye blank, but the other ablaze with some fell excitement. And straightway he burst into a low torrent of words, of which all I knew was that they were Italian, and therefore news of Raffles, if only I had known the language! But dumb-show might help us somewhat, and in I dragged him, though against his will, a new alarm in his one wild eye.

"Non capite?" he cried when I had him inside and had withstood the torrent.

"No, I'm bothered if I do!" I answered, guessing his question from his tone.

"Vostro amico," he repeated over and over again; and then, "Poco tempo, poco tempo, poco tempo!"

For once in my life the classical education of my public-school days was of real value. "My pal, my pal, and no time to be lost!" I translated freely, and flew for my hat.

"Ecco, signore!" cried the fellow, snatching the watch from my waistcoat pocket, and putting one black thumb-nail on the long hand, the other on he numeral twelve. "Mezzogiorno—poco tempo—poco tempo!" And again I seized his meaning, that it was twenty past eleven, and we must be there by twelve. But where, but where? It was maddening to be summoned like this, and not to know what had happened, nor to have any means of finding out. But my presence of mind stood by me still, I was improving by seven-league strides, and I crammed my handkerchief between the drum and hammer of the bell before leaving. The doctor could ring now till he was black in the face, but I was not coming, and he need not think it.

I half expected to find a hansom waiting, but there was none, and we had gone some distance down the Earl's Court Road before we got one; in fact, we had to run to the stand. Opposite is the church with the clock upon it, as everybody knows, and at sight of the dial my companion had wrung his hands; it was close upon the half-hour.

"Poco tempo—pochissimo!" he wailed. "Bloom-buree Ske-warr," he then cried to the cabman—"numero trentotto!"

"Bloomsbury Square," I roared on my own account, "I'll show you the house when we get there, only drive like be-damned!"

My companion lay back gasping in his corner. The small glass told me that my own face was pretty red.

"A nice show!" I cried; "and not a word can you tell me. Didn't you bring me a note?"

I might have known by this time that he had not, still I went through the pantomime of writing with my finger on my cuff. But he shrugged and shook his head.

"Niente," said he. "Una quistione di vita, di vita!"

"What's that?" I snapped, my early training come in again. "Say it slowly—andante—rallentando."

Thank Italy for the stage instructions in the songs one used to murder! The fellow actually understood.

"Una—quistione—di—vita."

"Or mors, eh?" I shouted, and up went the trap-door over our heads.

"Avanti, avanti, avanti!" cried the Italian, turning up his one-eyed face.

"Hell-to-leather," I translated, "and double fare if you do it by twelve o'clock."

But in the streets of London how is one to know the time? In the Earl's Court Road it had not been half-past, and at Barker's in High Street it was but a minute later. A long half-mile a minute, that was going like the wind, and indeed we had done much of it at a gallop. But the next hundred yards took us five minutes by the next clock, and which was one to believe? I fell back upon my own old watch (it was my own), which made it eighteen minutes to the hour as we swung across the Serpentine bridge, and by the quarter we were in the Bayswater Road—not up for once.

"Presto, presto," my pale guide murmured. "Affretatevi—avanti!"

"Ten bob if you do it," I cried through the trap, without the slightest notion of what we were to do. But it was "una quistione di vita," and "vostro amico" must and could only be my miserable Raffles.

What a very godsend is the perfect hansom to the man or woman in a hurry! It had been our great good fortune to jump into a perfect hansom; there was no choice, we had to take the first upon the rank, but it must have deserved its place with the rest nowhere. New tires, superb springs, a horse in a thousand, and a driver up to every trick of his trade! In and out we went like a fast half-back at the Rugby game, yet where the traffic was thinnest, there were we. And how he knew his way! At the Marble Arch he slipped out of the main stream, and so into Wigmore Street, then up and in and out and on until I saw the gold tips of the Museum palisade gleaming between the horse's ears in the sun. Plop, plop, plop; ting, ling, ling; bell and horse-shoes, horse-shoes and bell, until the colossal figure of C. J. Fox in a grimy toga spelt Bloomsbury Square with my watch still wanting three minutes to the hour.

"What number?" cried the good fellow over-head.

"Trentotto, trentotto," said my guide, but he was looking to the right, and I bundled him out to show the house on foot. I had not half-a-sovereign after all, but I flung our dear driver a whole one instead, and only wish that it had been a hundred.

Already the Italian had his latch-key in the door of 38, and in another moment we were rushing up the narrow stairs of as dingy a London house as prejudiced countryman can conceive. It was panelled, but it was dark and evil-smelling, and how we should have found our way even to the stairs but for an unwholesome jet of yellow gas in the hall, I cannot myself imagine. However, up we went pell-mell, to the right-about on the half-landing, and so like a whirlwind into the drawing-room a few steps higher. There the gas was also burning behind closed shutters, and the scene is photographed upon my brain, though I cannot have looked upon it for a whole instant as I sprang in at my leader's heels.

This room also was panelled, and in the middle of the wall on our left, his hands lashed to a ring-bolt high above his head, his toes barely touching the floor, his neck pinioned by a strap passing through smaller ring-bolts under either ear, and every inch of him secured on the same principle, stood, or rather hung, all that was left of Raffles, for at the first glance I believed him dead. A black ruler gagged him, the ends lashed behind his neck, the blood upon it caked to bronze in the gaslight. And in front of him, ticking like a sledge-hammer, its only hand upon the stroke of twelve, stood a simple, old-fashioned, grandfather's clock—but not for half an instant longer—only until my guide could hurl himself upon it and send the whole thing crashing into the corner. An ear-splitting report accompanied the crash, a white cloud lifted from the fallen clock, and I saw a revolver smoking in a vice screwed below the dial, an arrangement of wires sprouting from the dial itself, and the single hand at once at its zenith and in contact with these.

"Tumble to it, Bunny?"

He was alive; these were his first words; the Italian had the blood-caked ruler in his hand, and with his knife was reaching up to cut the thongs that lashed the hands. He was not tall enough, I seized him and lifted him up, then fell to work with my own knife upon the straps. And Raffles smiled faintly upon us through his blood-stains.

"I want you to tumble to it," he whispered; "the neatest thing in revenge I ever knew, and another minute would have fixed it. I've been waiting for it twelve hours, watching the clock round, death at the end of the lap! Electric connection. Simple enough. Hour-hand only—O Lord!"

We had cut the last strap. He could not stand. We supported him between us to a horsehair sofa, for the room was furnished, and I begged him not to speak, while his one-eyed deliverer was at the door before Raffles recalled him with a sharp word in Italian.

"He wants to get me a drink, but that can wait," said he, in firmer voice; "I shall enjoy it the more when I've told you what happened. Don't let him go, Bunny; put your back against the door. He's a decent soul, and it's lucky for me I got a word with him before they trussed me up. I've promised to set him up in life, and I will, but I don't want him out of my sight for the moment."

"If you squared him last night," I exclaimed, "why the blazes didn't he come to me till the eleventh hour?"

"Ah, I knew he'd have to cut it fine though I hoped not quite so fine as all that. But all's well that ends well, and I declare I don't feel so much the worse. I shall be sore about the gills for a bit—and what do you think?"

He pointed to the long black ruler with the bronze stain; it lay upon the floor; he held out his hand for it, and I gave it to him.

"THE SAME ONE I GAGGED him with," said Raffles, with his still ghastly smile; "he was a bit of an artist, old Corbucci, after all!"

"Now let's hear how you fell into his clutches," said I, briskly, for I was as anxious to hear as he seemed to tell me, only for my part I could have waited until we were safe in the flat.

"I do want to get it off my chest, Bunny," old Raffles admitted, "and yet I hardly can tell you after all. I followed your friend with the velvet eyes. I followed him all the way here. Of course I came up to have a good look at the house when he'd let himself in, and damme if he hadn't left the door ajar! Who could resist that? I had pushed it half open and had just one foot on the mat when I got such a crack on the head as I hope never to get again. When I came to my wits they were hauling me up to that ring-bolt by the hands, and old Corbucci himself was bowing to me, but how HE got here I don't know yet."

"I can tell you that," said I, and told how I had seen the Count for myself on the pavement underneath our windows. "Moreover," I continued, "I saw him spot you, and five minutes after in Earl's Court Road I was told he'd driven off in a cab. He would see you following his man, drive home ahead, and catch you by having the door left open in the way you describe."

"Well," said Raffles, "he deserved to catch me somehow, for he'd come from Naples on purpose, ruler and all, and the ring-bolts were ready fixed, and even this house taken furnished for nothing else! He meant catching me before he'd done, and scoring me off in exactly the same way that I scored off him, only going one better of course. He told me so himself, sitting where I am sitting now, at three o'clock this morning, and smoking a most abominable cigar that I've smelt ever since. It appears he sat twenty-four hours when I left HIM trussed up, but he said twelve would content him in my case, as there was certain death at the end of them, and I mightn't have life enough left to appreciate my end if he made it longer. But I wouldn't have trusted him if he could have got the clock to go twice round without firing off the pistol. He explained the whole mechanism of that to me; he had thought it all out on the vineyard I told you about; and then he asked if I remembered what he had promised me in the name of the Camorra. I only remembered some vague threats, but he was good enough to give me so many particulars of that institution that I could make a European reputation by exposing the whole show if it wasn't for my unfortunate resemblance to that infernal rascal Raffles. Do you think they would know me at the Yard, Bunny, after all this time? Upon my soul I've a good mind to risk it!"

I offered no opinion on the point. How could it interest me then? But interested I was in Raffles, never more so in my life. He had been tortured all night and half a day, yet he could sit and talk like this the moment we cut him down; he had been within a minute of his death, yet he was as full of life as ever; ill-treated and defeated at the best, he could still smile through his blood as though the boot were on the other leg. I had imagined that I knew my Raffles at last. I was not likely so to flatter myself again.

"But what has happened to these villains?" I burst out, and my indignation was not only against them for their cruelty, but also against their victim for his phlegmatic attitude toward them. It was difficult to believe that this was Raffles.

"Oh," said he, "they were to go off to Italy INSTANTER; they should be crossing now. But do listen to what I am telling you; it's interesting, my dear man. This old sinner Corbucci turns out to have been no end of a boss in the Camorra—says so himself. One of the capi paranze, my boy, no less; and the velvety Johnny a giovano onorato, Anglice, fresher. This fellow here was also in it, and I've sworn to protect him from them evermore; and it's just as I said, half the organ-grinders in London belong, and the whole lot of them were put on my tracks by secret instructions. This excellent youth manufactures iced poison on Saffron Hill when he's at home."

"And why on earth didn't he come to me quicker?"

"Because he couldn't talk to you, he could only fetch you, and it was as much as his life was worth to do that before our friends had departed. They were going by the eleven o'clock from Victoria, and that didn't leave much chance, but he certainly oughtn't to have run it as fine as he did. Still you must remember that I had to fix things up with him in the fewest possible words, in a single minute that the other two were indiscreet enough to leave us alone together."

The ragamuffin in question was watching us with all his solitary eye, as though he knew that we were discussing him. Suddenly he broke out in agonized accents, his hands clasped, and a face so full of fear that every moment I expected to see him on his knees. But Raffles answered kindly, reassuringly, I could tell from his tone, and then turned to me with a compassionate shrug.

"He says he couldn't find the mansions, Bunny, and really it's not to be wondered at. I had only time to tell him to hunt you up and bring you here by hook or crook before twelve to-day, and after all he has done that. But now the poor devil thinks you're riled with him, and that we'll give him away to the Camorra."

"Oh, it's not with him I'm riled," I said frankly, "but with those other blackguards, and—and with you, old chap, for taking it all as you do, while such infamous scoundrels have the last laugh, and are safely on their way to France!"

Raffles looked up at me with a curiously open eye, an eye that I never saw when he was not in earnest. I fancied he did not like my last expression but one. After all, it was no laughing matter to him.

"But are they?" said he. "I'm not so sure."

"You said they were!"

"I said they should be."

"Didn't you hear them go?"

"I heard nothing but the clock all night. It was like Big Ben striking at the last—striking nine to the fellow on the drop."

And in that open eye I saw at last a deep glimmer of the ordeal through which he had passed.

"But, my dear old Raffles, if they're still on the premises—"

The thought was too thrilling for a finished sentence.

"I hope they are," he said grimly, going to the door. "There's a gas on! Was that burning when you came in?"

Now that I thought of it, yes, it had been.

"And there's a frightfully foul smell," I added, as I followed Raffles down the stairs. He turned to me gravely with his hand upon the front-room door, and at the same moment I saw a coat with an astrakhan collar hanging on the pegs.

"They are in here, Bunny," he said, and turned the handle.

The door would only open a few inches. But a detestable odor came out, with a broad bar of yellow gaslight. Raffles put his handkerchief to his nose. I followed his example, signing to our ally to do the same, and in another minute we had all three squeezed into the room.

The man with the yellow boots was lying against the door, the Count's great carcass sprawled upon the table, and at a glance it was evident that both men had been dead some hours. The old Camorrist had the stem of a liqueur-glass between his swollen blue fingers, one of which had been cut in the breakage, and the livid flesh was also

E.W. HORNUNG

brown with the last blood that it would ever shed. His face was on the table, the huge moustache projecting from under either leaden cheek, yet looking itself strangely alive. Broken bread and scraps of frozen macaroni lay upon the cloth and at the bottom of two soup-plates and a tureen; the macaroni had a tinge of tomato; and there was a crimson dram left in the tumblers, with an empty fiasco to show whence it came. But near the great gray head upon the table another liqueur-glass stood, unbroken, and still full of some white and stinking liquid; and near that a tiny silver flask, which made me recoil from Raffles as I had not from the dead; for I knew it to be his.

"Come out of this poisonous air," he said sternly, "and I will tell you how it has happened."

So we all three gathered together in the hall. But it was Raffles who stood nearest the street-door, his back to it, his eyes upon us two. And though it was to me only that he spoke at first, he would pause from point to point, and translate into Italian for the benefit of the one-eyed alien to whom he owed his life.

"You probably don't even know the name, Bunny," he began, "of the deadliest poison yet known to science. It is cyanide of cacodyl, and I have carried that small flask of it about with me for months. Where I got it matters nothing; the whole point is that a mere sniff reduces flesh to clay. I have never had any opinion of suicide, as you know, but I always felt it worth while to be forearmed against the very worst. Well, a bottle of this stuff is calculated to stiffen an ordinary roomful of ordinary people within five minutes; and I remembered my flask when they had me as good as crucified in the small hours of this morning. I asked them to take it out of my pocket. I begged them to give me a drink before they left me. And what do you suppose they did?"

I thought of many things but suggested none, while Raffles turned this much of his statement into sufficiently fluent Italian. But when he faced me again his face was still flaming.

"That beast Corbucci!" said he—"how can I pity him? He took the flask; he would give me none; he flicked me in the face instead. My idea was that he, at least, should go with me—to sell my life as dearly as that—and a sniff would have settled us both. But no, he must tantalize and torment me; he thought it brandy; he must take it downstairs to drink to my destruction! Can you have any pity for a hound like that?"

"Let us go," I at last said, hoarsely, as Raffles finished speaking in Italian, and his second listener stood open-mouthed.

"We will go," said Raffles, "and we will chance being seen; if the worst comes to the worst this good chap will prove that I have been tied up since one o'clock this morning, and the medical evidence will decide how long those dogs have been dead."

But the worst did not come to the worst, more power to my unforgotten friend the cabman, who never came forward to say what manner of men he had driven to Bloomsbury Square at top speed on the very day upon which the tragedy was discovered there, or whence he had driven them. To be sure, they had not behaved like murderers, whereas the evidence at the inquest all went to show that the defunct Corbucci was little better. His reputation, which transpired with his identity, was that of a libertine and a renegade, while the infernal apparatus upstairs revealed the fiendish arts of the anarchist to boot. The inquiry resulted eventually in an open verdict, and was chiefly instrumental in killing such compassion as is usually felt for the dead who die in their sins.

But Raffles would not have passed this title for this tale.

To Catch a Thief

I

SOCIETY PERSONS ARE NOT LIKELY to have forgotten the series of audacious robberies by which so many of themselves suffered in turn during the brief course of a recent season. Raid after raid was made upon the smartest houses in town, and within a few weeks more than one exalted head had been shorn of its priceless tiara. The Duke and Duchess of Dorchester lost half the portable pieces of their historic plate on the very night of their Graces' almost equally historic costume ball. The Kenworthy diamonds were taken in broad daylight, during the excitement of a charitable meeting on the ground floor, and the gifts of her belted bridegroom to Lady May Paulton while the outer air was thick with a prismatic shower of confetti. It was obvious that all this was the work of no ordinary thief, and perhaps inevitable that the name of Raffles should have been dragged from oblivion by callous disrespecters of the departed and unreasoning apologists for the police. These wiseacres did not hesitate to bring a dead man back to life because they knew of no living one capable of such feats; it is their heedless and inconsequent calumnies that the present paper is partly intended to refute. As a matter of fact, our joint innocence in this matter was only exceeded by our common envy, and for a long time, like the rest of the world, neither of us had the slightest clew to the identity of the person who was following in our steps with such irritating results.

"I should mind less," said Raffles, "if the fellow were really playing my game. But abuse of hospitality was never one of my strokes, and it seems to me the only shot he's got. When we took old Lady Melrose's necklace, Bunny, we were not staying with the Melroses, if you recollect."

We were discussing the robberies for the hundredth time, but for once under conditions more favorable to animated conversation than our unique circumstances permitted in the flat. We did not often dine out. Dr. Theobald was one impediment, the risk of recognition was another. But there were exceptions, when the doctor was away or the patient defiant, and on these rare occasions we frequented a certain unpretentious restaurant in the Fulham quarter, where the cooking was plain but excellent, and the cellar a surprise. Our bottle of '89 champagne was empty to the label when the subject arose, to be touched by Raffles in the reminiscent manner indicated above. I can see his clear eye upon me now, reading me, weighing me. But I was not so sensitive to his scrutiny at the time. His tone was deliberate, calculating, preparatory; not as I heard it then, through a head full of wine, but as it floats back to me across the gulf between that moment and this.

"Excellent fillet!" said I, grossly. "So you think this chap is as much in society as we were, do you?"

I preferred not to think so myself. We had cause enough for jealousy without that. But Raffles raised his eyebrows an eloquent half-inch.

"As much, my dear Bunny? He is not only in it, but of it; there's no comparison between us there. Society is in rings like a target, and we never were in the bull's-eye, however thick you may lay on the ink! I was asked for my cricket. I haven't forgotten it yet. But this fellow's one of themselves, with the right of entre into the houses which we could only 'enter' in a professional sense. That's obvious unless all these little exploits are the work of different hands, which they as obviously are not. And it's why I'd give five hundred pounds to put salt on him to-night!"

"Not you," said I, as I drained my glass in festive incredulity.

"But I would, my dear Bunny. Waiter! another half-bottle of this," and Raffles leant across the table as the empty one was taken away. "I never was more serious in my life," he continued below his breath. "Whatever else our successor may be, he's not a dead man like me, or a marked man like you. If there's any truth in my theory he's one of the last people upon whom suspicion is ever likely to rest; and oh, Bunny, what a partner he would make for you and me!"

Under less genial influences the very idea of a third partner would have filled my soul with offence; but Raffles had chosen his moment unerringly, and his arguments lost nothing by the flowing accompaniment of the extra pint. They were, however, quite strong in themselves. The gist of them was that thus far we had remarkably little to show for what Raffles would call "our second innings." This even I could not deny. We had scored a few "long singles," but our "best shots" had gone "straight to hand," and we were "playing a deuced slow game." Therefore we needed a new partner—and the metaphor failed Raffles.

It had served its turn. I already agreed with him. In truth I was tired of my false position as hireling attendant, and had long fancied myself an object of suspicion to that other impostor the doctor. A fresh, untrammelled start was a fascinating idea to me, though two was company, and three in our case might be worse than none. But I did not see how we could hope, with our respective handicaps, to solve a problem which was already the despair of Scotland Yard.

"Suppose I have solved it," observed Raffles, cracking a walnut in his palm.

"How could you?" I asked, without believing for an instant that he had.

"I have been taking the Morning Post for some time now."

"Well?"

"You have got me a good many odd numbers of the less base society papers."

"I can't for the life of me see what you're driving at."

Raffles smiled indulgently as he cracked another nut.

"That's because you've neither observation nor imagination, Bunny— and yet you try to write! Well, you wouldn't think it, but I have a fairly complete list of the people who were at the various functions under cover of which these different little coups were brought off."

I said very stolidly that I did not see how that could help him. It was the only answer to his good-humored but self-satisfied contempt; it happened also to be true.

"Think," said Raffles, in a patient voice.

"When thieves break in and steal," said I, "upstairs, I don't see much point in discovering who was downstairs at the time."

"Quite," said Raffles—"when they do break in."

"But that's what they have done in all these cases. An upstairs door found screwed up, when things were at their height below; thief gone and jewels with him before alarm could be raised. Why, the trick's so old that I never knew you condescend to play it."

"Not so old as it looks," said Raffles, choosing the cigars and handing me mine. "Cognac or Benedictine, Bunny?"

"Brandy," I said, coarsely.

"Besides," he went on, "the rooms were not screwed up; at Dorchester House, at any rate, the door was only locked, and the key missing, so that it might have been done on either side."

"But that was where he left his rope-ladder behind him!" I exclaimed in triumph; but Raffles only shook his head.

"I don't believe in that rope-ladder, Bunny, except as a blind."

"Then what on earth do you believe?"

"That every one of these so-called burglaries has been done from the inside, by one of the guests; and what's more I'm very much mistaken if I haven't spotted the right sportsman."

I began to believe that he really had, there was such a wicked gravity in the eyes that twinkled faintly into mine. I raised my glass in convivial congratulation, and still remember the somewhat anxious eye with which Raffles saw it emptied.

"I can only find one likely name," he continued, "that figures in all these lists, and it is anything but a likely one at first sight. Lord Ernest Belville was at all those functions. Know anything about him, Bunny?"

"Not the Rational Drink fanatic?"

"Yes."

"That's all I want to know."

"Quite," said Raffles; "and yet what could be more promising? A man whose views are so broad and moderate, and so widely held already (saving your presence, Bunny), does not bore the world with them without ulterior motives. So far so good. What are this chap's motives? Does he want to advertise himself? No, he's somebody already. But is he rich? On the contrary, he's as poor as a rat for his position, and apparently without the least ambition to be anything else; certainly he won't enrich himself by making a public fad of what all sensible people are agreed upon as it is. Then suddenly one gets one's own old idea—the alternative profession! My cricket—his Rational Drink! But it is no use jumping to conclusions. I must know more than the newspapers can tell me. Our aristocratic friend is forty, and unmarried. What has he been doing all these years? How the devil was I to find out?"

"How did you?" I asked, declining to spoil my digestion with a conundrum, as it was his evident intention that I should.

"Interviewed him!" said Raffles, smiling slowly on my amazement.

"You—interviewed him?" I echoed. "When—and where?"

"Last Thursday night, when, if you remember, we kept early hours, because I felt done. What was the use of telling you what I had up my sleeve, Bunny? It might have ended in fizzle, as it still may. But Lord Ernest Belville was addressing the meeting at Exeter Hall; I waited for him when the show was over, dogged him home to King John's Mansions, and interviewed him in his own rooms there before he turned in."

My journalistic jealousy was piqued to the quick. Affecting a scepticism I did not feel (for no outrage was beyond the pale of his impudence), I inquired dryly which journal Raffles had pretended to represent. It is unnecessary to report his answer. I could not believe him without further explanation.

"I should have thought," he said, "that even you would have spotted a practice I never omit upon certain occasions. I always pay a visit to the drawing-room, and fill my waistcoat pocket from the card-tray. It is an immense help in any little temporary impersonation. On Thursday night I sent up the card of a powerful writer connected with a powerful paper; if Lord Ernest had known him in the flesh I should have been obliged to confess to a journalistic ruse; luckily he didn't—and I had been sent by my editor to get the interview for next morning. What could be better—for the alternative profession?"

I inquired what the interview had brought forth.

"Everything," said Raffles. "Lord Ernest has been a wanderer these twenty years. Texas, Fiji, Australia. I suspect him of wives and families in all three. But his manners are a liberal education. He gave me some beautiful whiskey, and forgot all about his fad. He is strong and subtle, but I talked him off his guard. He is going to the Kirkleathams' to-night—I saw the card stuck up. I stuck some wax into his keyhole as he was switching off the lights."

And, with an eye upon the waiters, Raffles showed me a skeleton key, newly twisted and filed; but my share of the extra pint (I am afraid no fair share) had made me dense. I looked from the key to Raffles with puckered forehead—for I happened to catch sight of it in the mirror behind him.

"The Dowager Lady Kirkleatham," he whispered, "has diamonds as big as beans, and likes to have 'em all on—and goes to bed early—and happens to be in town!"

And now I saw.

"The villain means to get them from her!"

"And I mean to get them from the villain," said Raffles; "or, rather, your share and mine."

"Will he consent to a partnership?"

"We shall have him at our mercy. He daren't refuse."

Raffles's plan was to gain access to Lord Ernest's rooms before midnight; there we were to lie in wait for the aristocratic rascal, and if I left all details to Raffles, and simply stood by in case of a rumpus, I should be playing my part and earning my share. It was a part that I had played before, not always with a good grace, though there had never been any question about the share. But to-night I was nothing loath. I had had just champagne enough—how Raffles knew my measure!— and I was ready and eager for anything. Indeed, I did not wish to wait for the coffee, which was to be especially strong by order of Raffles. But on that he insisted, and it was between ten and eleven when at last we were in our cab.

"It would be fatal to be too early," he said as we drove; "on the other hand, it would be dangerous to leave it too late. One must risk something. How I should love to drive down Piccadilly and see the lights! But unnecessary risks are another story."

II

KING JOHN'S MANSIONS, AS EVERYBODY knows, are the oldest, the ugliest, and the tallest block of flats in all London. But they are built upon a more generous scale than has since become the rule, and with a less studious regard for the economy of space. We were about to drive into the spacious courtyard when the gate-keeper checked us in order to let another hansom drive out.

It contained a middle-aged man of the military type, like ourselves in evening dress. That much I saw as his hansom crossed our bows, because I could not help seeing it, but I should not have given the incident a second thought if it had not been for his extraordinary effect upon Raffles. In an instant he was out upon the curb, paying the cabby, and in another he was leading me across the street, away from the mansions.

"Where on earth are you going?" I naturally exclaimed.

"Into the park," said he. "We are too early."

His voice told me more than his words. It was strangely stern.

"Was that him—in the hansom?"

"It was."

"Well, then, the coast's clear," said I, comfortably. I was for turning back then and there, but Raffles forced me on with a hand that hardened on my arm.

"It was a nearer thing than I care about," said he. "This seat will do; no, the next one's further from a lamp-post. We will give him a good half-hour, and I don't want to talk."

We had been seated some minutes when Big Ben sent a languid chime over our heads to the stars. It was half-past ten, and a sultry night.

Eleven had struck before Raffles awoke from his sullen reverie, and recalled me from mine with a slap on the back. In a couple of minutes we were in the lighted vestibule at the inner end of the courtyard of King John's Mansions.

"Just left Lord Ernest at Lady Kirkleatham's," said Raffles. "Gave me his key and asked us to wait for him in his rooms. Will you send us up in the lift?"

In a small way, I never knew old Raffles do anything better. There was not an instant's demur. Lord Ernest Belville's rooms were at the top of the building, but we were in them as quickly as lift could carry and page-boy conduct us. And there was no need for the skeleton key after all; the boy opened the outer door with one of his own, and switched on the lights before leaving us.

"Now that's interesting," said Raffles, as soon as we were alone; "they can come in and clean when he is out. What if he keeps his swag at the bank? By Jove, that's an idea for him! I don't believe he's getting rid of it; it's all lying low somewhere, if I'm not mistaken, and he's not a fool."

While he spoke he was moving about the sitting-room, which was charmingly furnished in the antique style, and making as many remarks as though he were an auctioneer's clerk with an inventory to prepare and a day to do it in, instead of a cracksman who might be surprised in his crib at any moment.

"Chippendale of sorts, eh, Bunny? Not genuine, of course; but where can you get genuine Chippendale now, and who knows it when they see it? There's no merit in mere antiquity. Yet the way people pose on the subject! If a thing's handsome and useful, and good cabinet-making, it's good enough for me."

"Hadn't we better explore the whole place?" I suggested nervously. He had not even bolted the outer door. Nor would he when I called his attention to the omission.

"If Lord Ernest finds his rooms locked up he'll raise Cain," said Raffles; "we must let him come in and lock up for himself before we corner him. But he won't come yet; if he did it might be awkward, for they'd tell him down below what I told them. A new staff comes on at midnight. I discovered that the other night."

"Supposing he does come in before?"

"Well, he can't have us turned out without first seeing who we are, and he won't try it on when I've had one word with him. Unless my suspicions are unfounded, I mean."

"Isn't it about time to test them?"

"My good Bunny, what do you suppose I've been doing all this while? He keeps nothing in here. There isn't a lock to the Chippendale that you couldn't pick with a penknife, and not a loose board in the floor, for I was treading for one before the boy left us. Chimney's no use in a place like this where they keep them swept for you. Yes, I'm quite ready to try his bedroom."

There was but a bathroom besides; no kitchen, no servant's room; neither are necessary in King John's Mansions. I thought it as well to put my head inside the bathroom while Raffles went into the bedroom, for I was tormented by the horrible idea that the man might all this time be concealed somewhere in the flat. But the bathroom blazed void in the electric light. I found Raffles hanging out of the starry square which was the bedroom window, for the room was still in darkness. I felt for the switch at the door.

"Put it out again!" said Raffles fiercely. He rose from the sill, drew blind and curtains carefully, then switched on the light himself. It fell upon a face creased more in pity than in anger, and Raffles only shook his head as I hung mine.

"It's all right, old boy," said he; "but corridors have windows too, and servants have eyes; and you and I are supposed to be in the other room, not in this. But cheer up, Bunny! This is THE room; look at the extra bolt on the door; he's had that put on, and there's an iron ladder to his window in case of fire! Way of escape ready against the hour of need; he's a better man than I thought him, Bunny, after all. But you may bet your bottom dollar that if there's any boodle in the flat it's in this room."

Yet the room was very lightly furnished; and nothing was locked. We looked everywhere, but we looked in vain. The wardrobe was filled with hanging coats and trousers in a press, the drawers with the softest silk and finest linen. It was a camp bedstead that would not have unsettled an anchorite; there was no place for treasure there. I looked up the chimney, but Raffles told me not to be a fool, and asked if I ever listened to what he said. There was no question about his temper now. I never knew him in a worse.

"Then he has got it in the bank," he growled. "I'll swear I'm not mistaken in my man!"

I had the tact not to differ with him there. But I could not help suggesting that now was our time to remedy any mistake we might have made. We were on the right side of midnight still.

"Then we stultify ourselves downstairs," said Raffles. "No, I'll be shot if I do! He may come in with the Kirkleatham diamonds! You do what you like, Bunny, but I don't budge."

"I certainly shan't leave you," I retorted, "to be knocked into the middle of next week by a better man than yourself."

I had borrowed his own tone, and he did not like it. They never do. I thought for a moment that Raffles was going to strike me—for the first and last time in his life. He could if he liked. My blood was up. I was ready to send him to the devil. And I emphasized my offence by nodding and shrugging toward a pair of very large Indian clubs that stood in the fender, on either side of the chimney up which I had presumed to glance.

In an instant Raffles had seized the clubs, and was whirling them about his gray head in a mixture of childish pique and puerile bravado which I should have thought him altogether above.

And suddenly as I watched him his face changed, softened, lit up, and he swung the clubs gently down upon the bed.

"They're not heavy enough for their size," said he rapidly; "and I'll take my oath they're not the same weight!"

He shook one club after the other, with both hands, close to his ear; then he examined their butt-ends under the electric light. I saw what he suspected now, and caught the contagion of his suppressed excitement. Neither of us spoke. But Raffles had taken out the portable tool-box that he called a knife, and always carried, and as he opened the gimlet he handed me the club he held. Instinctively I tucked the small end under my arm, and presented the other to Raffles.

"Hold him tight," he whispered, smiling. "He's not only a better man than I thought him, Bunny; he's hit upon a better dodge than ever I did, of its kind. Only I should have weighted them evenly—to a hair."

He had screwed the gimlet into the circular butt, close to the edge, and now we were wrenching in opposite directions. For a moment or more nothing happened. Then all at once something gave, and Raffles swore an oath as soft as any prayer. And for the minute after that his hand went round and round with the gimlet, as though he were grinding a piano-organ, while the end wormed slowly out on its delicate thread of fine hard wood.

The clubs were as hollow as drinking-horns, the pair of them, for we went from one to the other without pausing to undo the padded packets that poured out upon the bed. These were deliciously heavy to the hand, yet thickly swathed in cotton-wool, so that some stuck together, retaining the shape of the cavity, as though they had been run out of a mould. And when we did open them—but let Raffles speak.

He had deputed me to screw in the ends of the clubs, and to replace the latter in the fender where we had found them. When I had done the counterpane was glittering with diamonds where it was not shimmering with pearls.

"If this isn't that tiara that Lady May was married in," said Raffles, "and that disappeared out of the room she changed in, while it rained confetti on the steps, I'll present it to her instead of the one she lost. . . It was stupid to keep these old gold spoons, valuable as they are; they made the difference in the weight. . . Here we have probably the Kenworthy diamonds. . . I don't know the history of these pearls. . . This looks like one family of rings—left on the basin-stand, perhaps—alas, poor lady! And that's the lot."

Our eyes met across the bed.

"What's it all worth?" I asked, hoarsely.

"Impossible to say. But more than all we ever took in all our lives. That I'll swear to."

"More than all—"

My tongue swelled with the thought.

"But it'll take some turning into cash, old chap!"

"And—must it be a partnership?" I asked, finding a lugubrious voice at length.

"Partnership be damned!" cried Raffles, heartily. "Let's get out quicker than we came in."

We pocketed the things between us, cotton-wool and all, not because we wanted the latter, but to remove all immediate traces of our really meritorious deed.

"The sinner won't dare to say a word when he does find out," remarked Raffles of Lord Ernest; "but that's no reason why he should find out before he must. Everything's straight in here, I think; no, better leave the window open as it was, and the blind up. Now out with the light. One peep at the other room. That's all right, too. Out with the passage light, Bunny, while I open—"

His words died away in a whisper. A key was fumbling at the lock outside.

"Out with it—out with it!" whispered Raffles in an agony; and as

I obeyed he picked me off my feet and swung me bodily but silently into the bedroom, just as the outer door opened, and a masterful step strode in.

The next five were horrible minutes. We heard the apostle of Rational Drink unlock one of the deep drawers in his antique sideboard, and sounds followed suspiciously like the splash of spirits and the steady stream from a siphon. Never before or since did I experience such a thirst as assailed me at that moment, nor do I believe that many tropical explorers have known its equal. But I had Raffles with me, and his hand was as steady and as cool as the hand of a trained nurse. That I know because he turned up the collar of my overcoat for me, for some reason, and buttoned it at the throat. I afterwards found that he had done the same to his own, but I did not hear him doing it. The one thing I heard in the bedroom was a tiny metallic click, muffled and deadened in his overcoat pocket, and it not only removed my last tremor, but strung me to a higher pitch of excitement than ever. Yet I had then no conception of the game that Raffles was deciding to play, and that I was to play with him in another minute.

It cannot have been longer before Lord Ernest came into his bedroom. Heavens, but my heart had not forgotten how to thump! We were standing near the door, and I could swear he touched me; then his boots creaked, there was a rattle in the fender—and Raffles switched on the light.

Lord Ernest Belville crouched in its glare with one Indian club held by the end, like a footman with a stolen bottle. A good-looking, well-built, iron-gray, iron-jawed man; but a fool and a weakling at that moment, if he had never been either before.

"Lord Ernest Belville," said Raffles, "it's no use. This is a loaded revolver, and if you force me I shall use it on you as I would on any other desperate criminal. I am here to arrest you for a series of robberies at the Duke of Dorchester's, Sir John Kenworthy's, and other noblemen's and gentlemen's houses during the present season. You'd better drop what you've got in your hand. It's empty."

Lord Ernest lifted the club an inch or two, and with it his eyebrows—and after it his stalwart frame as the club crashed back into the fender. And as he stood at his full height, a courteous but ironic smile under the cropped moustache, he looked what he was, criminal or not.

"Scotland Yard?" said he.

"That's our affair, my lord."

"I didn't think they'd got it in them," said Lord Ernest. "Now I recognize you. You're my interviewer. No, I didn't think any of you fellows had got all that in you. Come into the other room, and I'll show you something else. Oh, keep me covered by all means. But look at this!"

On the antique sideboard, their size doubled by reflection in the polished mahogany, lay a coruscating cluster of precious stones, that fell in festoons about Lord Ernest's fingers as he handed them to Raffles with scarcely a shrug.

"The Kirkleatham diamonds," said he. "Better add 'em to the bag."

Raffles did so without a smile; with his overcoat buttoned up to the chin, his tall hat pressed down to his eyes, and between the two his incisive features and his keen, stern glance, he looked the ideal detective of fiction and the stage. What *I* looked God knows, but I did my best to glower and show my teeth at his side. I had thrown myself into the game, and it was obviously a winning one.

"Wouldn't take a share, I suppose?" Lord Ernest said casually.

Raffles did not condescend to reply. I rolled back my lips like a bull-pup.

"Then a drink, at least!"

My mouth watered, but Raffles shook his head impatiently.

"We must be going, my lord, and you will have to come with us."

I wondered what in the world we should do with him when we had got him.

"Give me time to put some things together? Pair of pyjamas and tooth-brush, don't you know?"

"I cannot give you many minutes, my lord, but I don't want to cause a disturbance here, so I'll tell them to call a cab if you like. But I shall be back in a minute, and you must be ready in five. Here, inspector, you'd better keep this while I am gone."

And I was left alone with that dangerous criminal! Raffles nipped my arm as he handed me the revolver, but I got small comfort out of that.

"'Sea-green Incorruptible?'" inquired Lord Ernest as we stood face to face.

"You don't corrupt me," I replied through naked teeth.

"Then come into my room. I'll lead the way. Think you can hit me if I misbehave?"

I put the bed between us without a second's delay. My prisoner flung a suit-case upon it, and tossed things into it with a dejected air;

suddenly, as he was fitting them in, without raising his head (which I was watching), his right hand closed over the barrel with which I covered him.

"You'd better not shoot," he said, a knee upon his side of the bed; "if you do it may be as bad for you as it will be for me!"

I tried to wrest the revolver from him.

"I will if you force me," I hissed.

"You'd better not," he repeated, smiling; and now I saw that if I did I should only shoot into the bed or my own legs. His hand was on the top of mine, bending it down, and the revolver with it. The strength of it was as the strength of ten of mine; and now both his knees were on the bed; and suddenly I saw his other hand, doubled into a fist, coming up slowly over the suit-case.

"Help!" I called feebly.

"Help, forsooth! I begin to believe You Are from the Yard," he said— and his upper-cut came with the "Yard." It caught me under the chin.

It lifted me off my legs. I have a dim recollection of the crash that I made in falling.

III

Raffles was standing over me when I recovered consciousness. I lay stretched upon the bed across which that blackguard Belville had struck his knavish blow. The suit-case was on the floor, but its dastardly owner had disappeared.

"Is he gone?" was my first faint question.

"Thank God you're not, anyway!" replied Raffles, with what struck me then as mere flippancy. I managed to raise myself upon one elbow.

"I meant Lord Ernest Belville," said I, with dignity. "Are you quite sure that he's cleared out?"

Raffles waved a hand towards the window, which stood wide open to the summer stars.

"Of course," said he, "and by the route I intended him to take; he's gone by the iron-ladder, as I hoped he would. What on earth should we have done with him? My poor, dear Bunny, I thought you'd take a bribe! But it's really more convincing as it is, and just as well for Lord Ernest to be convinced for the time being."

"Are you sure he is?" I questioned, as I found a rather shaky pair of legs.

"Of course!" cried Raffles again, in the tone to make one blush for the least misgiving on the point. "Not that it matters one bit," he added, airily, "for we have him either way; and when he does tumble to it, as he may any minute, he won't dare to open his mouth."

"Then the sooner we clear out the better," said I, but I looked askance at the open window, for my head was spinning still.

"When you feel up to it," returned Raffles, "we shall STROLL out, and I shall do myself the honor of ringing for the lift. The force of habit is too strong in you, Bunny. I shall shut the window and leave everything exactly as we found it. Lord Ernest will probably tumble before he is badly missed; and then he may come back to put salt on us; but I should like to know what he can do even if he succeeds! Come, Bunny, pull yourself together, and you'll be a different man when you're in the open air."

And for a while I felt one, such was my relief at getting out of those infernal mansions with unfettered wrists; this we managed easily enough; but once more Raffles's performance of a small part was no less perfect than his more ambitious work upstairs, and something of the successful artist's elation possessed him as we walked arm-in-arm across St. James's Park. It was long since I had known him so pleased with himself, and only too long since he had had such reason.

"I don't think I ever had a brighter idea in my life," he said; "never thought of it till he was in the next room; never dreamt of its coming off so ideally even then, and didn't much care, because we had him all ways up. I'm only sorry you let him knock you out. I was waiting outside the door all the time, and it made me sick to hear it. But I once broke my own head, Bunny, if you remember, and not in half such an excellent cause!"

Raffles touched all his pockets in his turn, the pockets that contained a small fortune apiece, and he smiled in my face as we crossed the lighted avenues of the Mall. Next moment he was hailing a hansom— for I suppose I was still pretty pale—and not a word would he let me speak until we had alighted as near as was prudent to the flat.

"What a brute I've been, Bunny!" he whispered then, "but you take half the swag, old boy, and right well you've earned it. No, we'll go in by the wrong door and over the roof; it's too late for old Theobald to be still at the play, and too early for him to be safely in his cups."

So we climbed the many stairs with cat-like stealth, and like cats crept out upon the grimy leads. But to-night they were no blacker than their canopy of sky; not a chimney-stack stood out against the starless night; one had to feel one's way in order to avoid tripping over the low parapets of the L-shaped wells that ran from roof to basement to light the inner rooms. One of these wells was spanned by a flimsy bridge with iron handrails that felt warm to the touch as Raffles led the way across! A hotter and a closer night I have never known.

"The flat will be like an oven," I grumbled, at the head of our own staircase.

"Then we won't go down," said Raffles, promptly; "we'll slack it up here for a bit instead. No, Bunny, you stay where you are! I'll fetch you a drink and a deck-chair, and you shan't come down till you feel more fit."

And I let him have his way, I will not say as usual, for I had even less than my normal power of resistance that night. That villainous upper-cut! My head still sang and throbbed, as I seated myself on one of the aforesaid parapets, and buried it in my hot hands. Nor was the night one to dispel a headache; there was distinct thunder in the air. Thus I sat in a heap, and brooded over my misadventure, a pretty figure of a subordinate villain, until the step came for which I waited; and it never struck me that it came from the wrong direction.

"You have been quick," said I, simply.

"Yes," hissed a voice I recognized; "and you've got to be quicker still! Here, out with your wrists; no, one at a time; and if you utter a syllable you're a dead man."

It was Lord Ernest Belville; his close-cropped, iron-gray moustache gleamed through the darkness, drawn up over his set teeth. In his hand glittered a pair of handcuffs, and before I knew it one had snapped its jaws about my right wrist.

"Now come this way," said Lord Ernest, showing me a revolver also, "and wait for your friend. And, recollect, a single syllable of warning will be your death!"

With that the ruffian led me to the very bridge I had just crossed at Raffles's heels, and handcuffed me to the iron rail midway across the chasm. It no longer felt warm to my touch, but icy as the blood in all my veins.

So this high-born hypocrite had beaten us at our game and his, and Raffles had met his match at last! That was the most intolerable thought, that Raffles should be down in the flat on my account, and that I could not warn him of his impending fate; for how was it possible without making such an outcry as should bring the mansions about our ears?

And there I shivered on that wretched plank, chained like Andromeda to the rock, with a black infinity above and below; and before my eyes, now grown familiar with the peculiar darkness, stood Lord Ernest Belville, waiting for Raffles to emerge with full hands and unsuspecting heart! Taken so horribly unawares, even Raffles must fall an easy prey to a desperado in resource and courage scarcely second to himself, but one whom he had fatally underrated from the beginning. Not that I paused to think how the thing had happened; my one concern was for what was to happen next.

And what did happen was worse than my worst foreboding, for first a light came flickering into the sort of companion-hatch at the head of the stairs, and finally Raffles—in his shirt-sleeves! He was not only carrying a candle to put the finishing touch to him as a target; he had dispensed with coat and waistcoat downstairs, and was at once full-handed and unarmed.

"Where are you, old chap?" he cried, softly, himself blinded by the light he carried; and he advanced a couple of steps towards Belville. "This isn't you, is it?"

And Raffles stopped, his candle held on high, a folding chair under the other arm.

"No, I am not your friend," replied Lord Ernest, easily; "but kindly remain standing exactly where you are, and don't lower that candle an inch, unless you want your brains blown into the street."

Raffles said never a word, but for a moment did as he was bid; and the unshaken flame of the candle was testimony alike to the stillness of the night and to the finest set of nerves in Europe.

Then, to my horror, he coolly stooped, placing candle and chair on the leads, and his hands in his pockets, as though it were but a popgun that covered him.

"Why didn't you shoot?" he asked insolently as he rose. "Frightened of the noise? I should be, too, with an old-pattern machine like that. All very well for service in the field—but on the house-tops at dead of night!"

"I shall shoot, however," replied Lord Ernest, as quietly in his turn, and with less insolence, "and chance the noise, unless you instantly restore my property. I am glad you don't dispute the last word," he continued after a slight pause. "There is no keener honor than that which subsists, or ought to subsist, among thieves; and I need hardly say that I soon spotted you as one of the fraternity. Not in the beginning, mind you! For the moment I did think you were one of these smart detectives jumped to life from some sixpenny magazine; but to preserve the illusion you ought to provide yourself with a worthier lieutenant. It was he who gave your show away," chuckled the wretch, dropping for a moment the affected style of speech which seemed intended to enhance our humiliation; "smart detectives don't go about with little innocents to assist them. You needn't be anxious about him, by the way; it wasn't necessary to pitch him into the street; he is to be seen though not heard, if you look in the right direction. Nor must you put all the blame upon your friend; it was not he, but you, who made so sure that I had got out by the window. You see, I was in my bathroom all the time—with the door open."

"The bathroom, eh?" Raffles echoed with professional interest. "And you followed us on foot across the park?"

"Of course."

"And then in a cab?"

"And afterwards on foot once more."

"The simplest skeleton would let you in down below."

I saw the lower half of Lord Ernest's face grinning in the light of the candle set between them on the ground.

"You follow every move," said he; "there can be no doubt you are one of the fraternity; and I shouldn't wonder if we had formed our style upon the same model. Ever know A. J. Raffles?"

The abrupt question took my breath away; but Raffles himself did not lose an instant over his answer.

"Intimately," said he.

"That accounts for you, then," laughed Lord Ernest, "as it does for me, though I never had the honor of the master's acquaintance. Nor is it for me to say which is the worthier disciple. Perhaps, however, now that your friend is handcuffed in mid-air, and you yourself are at my mercy, you will concede me some little temporary advantage?"

And his face split in another grin from the cropped moustache downward, as I saw no longer by candlelight but by a flash of lightning which tore the sky in two before Raffles could reply.

"You have the bulge at present," admitted Raffles; "but you have still to lay hands upon your, or our, ill-gotten goods. To shoot me is not necessarily to do so; to bring either one of us to a violent end is only to court a yet more violent and infinitely more disgraceful one for yourself. Family considerations alone should rule that risk out of your game. Now, an hour or two ago, when the exact opposite—"

The remainder of Raffles's speech was drowned from my ears by the belated crash of thunder which the lightning had foretold. So loud, however, was the crash when it came, that the storm was evidently approaching us at a high velocity; yet as the last echo rumbled away, I heard Raffles talking as though he had never stopped.

"You offered us a share," he was saying; "unless you mean to murder us both in cold blood, it will be worth your while to repeat that offer. We should be dangerous enemies; you had far better make the best of us as friends."

"Lead the way down to your flat," said Lord Ernest, with a flourish of his service revolver, "and perhaps we may talk about it. It is for me to make the terms, I imagine, and in the first place I am not going to get wet to the skin up here."

The rain was beginning in great drops, even as he spoke, and by a second flash of lightning I saw Raffles pointing to me.

"But what about my friend?" said he.

And then came the second peal.

"Oh, HE's all right," the great brute replied; "do him good! You don't catch me letting myself in for two to one!"

"You will find it equally difficult," rejoined Raffles, "to induce me to leave my friend to the mercy of a night like this. He has not recovered from the blow you struck him in your own rooms. I am not such a fool as to blame you for that, but you are a worse sportsman than I take you for if you think of leaving him where he is. If he stays, however, so do I."

And, just as it ceased, Raffles's voice seemed distinctly nearer to me; but in the darkness and the rain, which was now as heavy as hail, I could see nothing clearly. The rain had already extinguished the candle. I heard an oath from Belville, a laugh from Raffles, and for a second that was all. Raffles was coming to me, and the other could not even see to fire; that was all I knew in the pitchy interval of invisible rain before the next crash and the next flash.

And then!

This time they came together, and not till my dying hour shall I forget the sight that the lightning lit and the thunder applauded. Raffles was on one of the parapets of the gulf that my foot-bridge spanned, and in the sudden illumination he stepped across it as one might across a garden path. The width was scarcely greater, but the depth! In the sudden flare I saw to the concrete bottom of the well, and it looked no larger than the hollow of my hand. Raffles was laughing in my ear;

he had the iron railing fast; it was between us, but his foothold was as secure as mine. Lord Ernest Belville, on the contrary, was the fifth of a second late for the light, and half a foot short in his spring. Something struck our plank bridge so hard as to set it quivering like a harp-string; there was half a gasp and half a sob in mid-air beneath our feet; and then a sound far below that I prefer not to describe. I am not sure that I could hit upon the perfect simile; it is more than enough for me that I can hear it still. And with that sickening sound came the loudest clap of thunder yet, and a great white glare that showed us our enemy's body far below, with one white hand spread like a starfish, but the head of him mercifully twisted underneath.

"It was all his own fault, Bunny. Poor devil! May he and all of us be forgiven; but pull yourself together for your own sake. Well, you can't fall; stay where you are a minute."

I remember the uproar of the elements while Raffles was gone; no other sound mingled with it; not the opening of a single window, not the uplifting of a single voice. Then came Raffles with soap and water, and the gyve was wheedled from one wrist, as you withdraw a ring for which the finger has grown too large. Of the rest, I only remember shivering till morning in a pitch-dark flat, whose invalid occupier was for once the nurse, and I his patient.

And that is the true ending of the episode in which we two set ourselves to catch one of our own kidney, albeit in another place I have shirked the whole truth. It is not a grateful task to show Raffles as completely at fault as he really was on that occasion; nor do I derive any subtle satisfaction from recounting my own twofold humiliation, or from having assisted never so indirectly in the death of a not uncongenial sinner. The truth, however, has after all a merit of its own, and the great kinsfolk of poor Lord Ernest have but little to lose by its divulgence. It would seem that they knew more of the real character of the apostle of Rational Drink than was known at Exeter Hall. The tragedy was indeed hushed up, as tragedies only are when they occur in such circles. But the rumor that did get abroad, as to the class of enterprise which the poor scamp was pursuing when he met his death, cannot be too soon exploded, since it breathed upon the fair fame of some of the most respectable flats in Kensington.

An Old Flame

I

THE SQUARE SHALL BE NAMELESS, but if you drive due west from Piccadilly the cab-man will eventually find it on his left, and he ought to thank you for two shillings. It is not a fashionable square, but there are few with a finer garden, while the studios on the south side lend distinction of another sort. The houses, however, are small and dingy, and about the last to attract the expert practitioner in search of a crib. Heaven knows it was with no such thought I trailed Raffles thither, one unlucky evening at the latter end of that same season, when Dr. Theobald had at last insisted upon the bath-chair which I had foreseen in the beginning. Trees whispered in the green garden aforesaid, and the cool, smooth lawns looked so inviting that I wondered whether some philanthropic resident could not be induced to lend us the key. But Raffles would not listen to the suggestion, when I stopped to make it, and what was worse, I found him looking wistfully at the little houses instead.

"Such balconies, Bunny! A leg up, and there you would be!"

I expressed a conviction that there would be nothing worth taking in the square, but took care to have him under way again as I spoke.

"I daresay you're right," sighed Raffles. "Rings and watches, I suppose, but it would be hard luck to take them from people who live in houses like these. I don't know, though. Here's one with an extra story. Stop, Bunny; if you don't stop I'll hold on to the railings! This is a good house; look at the knocker and the electric bell. They've had that put in. There's some money here, my rabbit! I dare bet there's a silver-table in the drawing-room; and the windows are wide open. Electric light, too, by Jove!"

Since stop I must, I had done so on the other side of the road, in the shadow of the leafy palings, and as Raffles spoke the ground floor windows opposite had flown alight, showing as pretty a little dinner-table as one could wish to see, with a man at his wine at the far end, and the back of a lady in evening dress toward us. It was like a lantern-picture thrown upon a screen. There were only the pair of them, but the table was brilliant with silver and gay with flowers, and the maid waited with the indefinable air of a good servant. It certainly seemed a good house.

"She's going to let down the blind!" whispered Raffles, in high excitement. "No, confound them, they've told her not to. Mark down her necklace, Bunny, and invoice his stud. What a brute he looks! But I like the table, and that's her show. She has the taste; but he must have money. See the festive picture over the sideboard? Looks to me like a Jacques Saillard. But that silver-table would be good enough for me."

"Get on," said I. "You're in a bath-chair."

"But the whole square's at dinner! We should have the ball at our feet. It wouldn't take two twos!"

"With those blinds up, and the cook in the kitchen underneath?"

He nodded, leaning forward in the chair, his hands upon the wraps about his legs.

"You must be mad," said I, and got back to my handles with the word, but when I tugged the chair ran light.

"Keep an eye on the rug," came in a whisper from the middle of the road; and there stood my invalid, his pale face in a quiver of pure mischief, yet set with his insane resolve. "I'm only going to see whether that woman has a silver-table—"

"We don't want it—"

"It won't take a minute—"

"It's madness, madness—"

"Then don't you wait!"

It was like him to leave me with that, and this time I had taken him at his last word had not my own given me an idea. Mad I had called him, and mad I could declare him upon oath if necessary. It was not as though the thing had happened far from home. They could learn all about us at the nearest mansions. I referred them to Dr. Theobald; this was a Mr. Maturin, one of his patients, and I was his keeper, and he had never given me the slip before. I heard myself making these explanations on the doorstep, and pointing to the deserted bath-chair as the proof, while the pretty parlor maid ran for the police. It would be a more serious matter for me than for my charge. I should lose my place. No, he had never done such a thing before, and I would answer for it that he never should again.

I saw myself conducting Raffles back to his chair, with a firm hand and a stern tongue. I heard him thanking me in whispers on the way home. It would be the first tight place I had ever got him out of, and I was quite anxious for him to get into it, so sure was I of every move. My whole position had altered in the few seconds that it took me to follow this illuminating train of ideas; it was now so strong that I could watch Raffles without much anxiety. And he was worth watching.

He had stepped boldly but softly to the front door, and there he was still waiting, ready to ring if the door opened or a face appeared in the area, and doubtless to pretend that he had rung already. But he had not to ring at all; and suddenly I saw his foot in the letter-box, his left hand on the lintel overhead. It was thrilling, even to a hardened accomplice with an explanation up his sleeve! A tight grip with that left hand of his, as he leant backward with all his weight upon those five fingers; a right arm stretched outward and upward to its last inch; and the base of the low, projecting balcony was safely caught.

I looked down and took breath. The maid was removing the crumbs in the lighted room, and the square was empty as before. What a blessing it was the end of the season! Many of the houses remained in darkness. I looked up again, and Raffles was drawing his left leg over the balcony railing. In another moment he had disappeared through one of the French windows which opened upon the balcony, and in yet another he had switched on the electric light within. This was bad enough, for now I, at least, could see everything he did; but the crowning folly was still to come. There was no point in it; the mad thing was done for my benefit, as I knew at once and he afterward confessed; but the lunatic reappeared on the balcony, bowing like a mountebank— in his crape mask!

I set off with the empty chair, but I came back. I could not desert old Raffles, even when I would, but must try to explain away his mask as well, if he had not the sense to take it off in time. It would be difficult, but burglaries are not usually committed from a bath-chair, and for the rest I put my faith in Dr. Theobald. Meanwhile Raffles had at least withdrawn from the balcony, and now I could only see his head as he peered into a cabinet at the other side of the room. It was like the opera of Aida, in which two scenes are enacted simultaneously, one in the dungeon below, the other in the temple above. In the same fashion my attention now became divided between the picture of Raffles moving stealthily about the upper room, and that of the husband and wife at table underneath. And all at once, as the man replenished his glass with a shrug of the shoulders, the woman pushed back her chair and sailed to the door.

Raffles was standing before the fireplace upstairs. He had taken one of the framed photographs from the chimney-piece, and was scanning it at suicidal length through the eye-holes in the hideous mask which he still wore. He would need it after all. The lady had left the room below, opening and shutting the door for herself; the man was filling his glass once more. I would have shrieked my warning to Raffles, so fatally engrossed overhead, but at this moment (of all others) a constable (of all men) was marching sedately down our side of the square. There was nothing for it but to turn a melancholy eye upon the bath-chair, and to ask the constable the time. I was evidently to be kept there all night, I remarked, and only realized with the words that they disposed of my other explanations before they were uttered. It was a horrible moment for such a discovery. Fortunately the enemy was on the pavement, from which he could scarcely have seen more than the drawing-room ceiling, had he looked; but he was not many houses distant when a door opened and a woman gasped so that I heard both across the road. And never shall I forget the subsequent tableaux in the lighted room behind the low balcony and the French windows.

Raffles stood confronted by a dark and handsome woman whose profile, as I saw it first in the electric light, is cut like a cameo in my memory. It had the undeviating line of brow and nose, the short upper lip, the perfect chin, that are united in marble oftener than in the flesh; and like marble she stood, or rather like some beautiful pale bronze; for that was her coloring, and she lost none of it that I could see, neither trembled; but her bosom rose and fell, and that was all. So she stood without flinching before a masked ruffian, who, I felt, would be the first to appreciate her courage; to me it was so superb that I could think of it in this way even then, and marvel how Raffles himself could stand unabashed before so brave a figure. He had not to do so long. The woman scorned him, and he stood unmoved, a framed photograph still in his hand. Then, with a quick, determined movement she turned, not to the door or to the bell, but to the open window by which Raffles had entered; and this with that accursed policeman still in view. So far no word had passed between the pair. But at this point Raffles said something, I could not hear what, but at the sound of his voice the woman wheeled. And Raffles was looking humbly in her face, the crape mask snatched from his own.

"Arthur!" she cried; and that might have been heard in the middle of the square garden.

Then they stood gazing at each other, neither unmoved any more, and while they stood the street-door opened and banged. It was her husband leaving the house, a fine figure of a man, but a dissipated face, and a step even now distinguished by the extreme caution which precedes unsteadiness. He broke the spell. His wife came to the balcony, then looked back into the room, and yet again along the road, and this time I saw her face. It was the face of one glancing indeed from Hyperion to a satyr. And then I saw the rings flash, as her hand fell gently upon Raffles's arm.

They disappeared from that window. Their heads showed for an instant in the next. Then they dipped out of sight, and an inner ceiling flashed out under a new light; they had gone into the back drawing-room, beyond my ken. The maid came up with coffee, her mistress hastily met her at the door, and once more disappeared. The square was as quiet as ever. I remained some minutes where I was. Now and then I thought I heard their voices in the back drawing-room. I was seldom sure.

My state of mind may be imagined by those readers who take an interest in my personal psychology. It does not amuse me to look back upon it. But at length I had the sense to put myself in Raffles's place. He had been recognized at last, he had come to life. Only one person knew as yet, but that person was a woman, and a woman who had once been fond of him, if the human face could speak. Would she keep his secret? Would he tell her where he lived? It was terrible to think we were such neighbors, and with the thought that it was terrible came a little enlightenment as to what could still be done for the best. He would not tell her where he lived. I knew him too well for that. He would run for it when he could, and the bath-chair and I must not be there to give him away. I dragged the infernal vehicle round the nearer corner. Then I waited—there could be no harm in that—and at last he came.

He was walking briskly, so I was right, and he had not played the invalid to her; yet I heard him cry out with pleasure as he turned the corner, and he flung himself into the chair with a long-drawn sigh that did me good.

"Well done, Bunny—well done! I am on my way to Earl's Court, she's capable of following me, but she won't look for me in a bath-chair. Home, home, home, and not another word till we get there!"

Capable of following him? She overtook us before we were past the studios on the south side of the square, the woman herself, in a hooded opera-cloak. But she never gave us a glance, and we saw her turn safely in the right direction for Earl's Court, and the wrong one for

E. W. HORNUNG

our humble mansions. Raffles thanked his gods in a voice that trembled, and five minutes later we were in the flat. Then for once it was Raffles who filled the tumblers and found the cigarettes, and for once (and once only in all my knowledge of him) did he drain his glass at a draught.

"You didn't see the balcony scene?" he asked at length; and they were his first words since the woman passed us on his track.

"Do you mean when she came in?"

"No, when I came down."

"I didn't."

"I hope nobody else saw it," said Raffles devoutly. "I don't say that Romeo and Juliet were brother and sister to us. But you might have said so, Bunny!"

He was staring at the carpet with as wry a face as lover ever wore.

"An old flame?" said I, gently.

"A married woman," he groaned.

"So I gathered."

"But she always was one, Bunny," said he, ruefully. "That's the trouble. It makes all the difference in the world!"

I saw the difference, but said I did not see how it could make any now. He had eluded the lady, after all; had we not seen her off upon a scent as false as scent could be? There was occasion for redoubled caution in the future, but none for immediate anxiety. I quoted the bedside Theobald, but Raffles did not smile. His eyes had been downcast all this time, and now, when he raised them, I perceived that my comfort had been administered to deaf ears.

"Do you know who she is?" said he.

"Not from Eve."

"Jacques Saillard," he said, as though now I must know.

But the name left me cold and stolid. I had heard it, but that was all. It was lamentable ignorance, I am aware, but I had specialized in Letters at the expense of Art.

"You must know her pictures," said Raffles, patiently; "but I suppose you thought she was a man. They would appeal to you, Bunny; that festive piece over the sideboard was her work. Sometimes they risk her at the Academy, sometimes they fight shy. She has one of those studios in the same square; they used to live up near Lord's."

My mind was busy brightening a dim memory of nymphs reflected in woody pools. "Of course!" I exclaimed, and added something about "a clever woman." Raffles rose at the phrase.

"A clever woman!" he echoed, scornfully; "if she were only that I should feel safe as houses. Clever women can't forget their cleverness, they carry it as badly as a boy does his wine, and are about as dangerous. I don't call Jacques Saillard clever outside her art, but neither do I call her a woman at all. She does man's work over a man's name, has the will of any ten men I ever knew, and I don't mind telling you that I fear her more than any person on God's earth. I broke with her once," said Raffles, grimly, "but I know her. If I had been asked to name the one person in London by whom I was keenest Not to be bowled out, I should have named Jacques Saillard."

That he had never before named her to me was as characteristic as the reticence with which Raffles spoke of their past relations, and even of their conversation in the back drawing-room that evening.

It was a question of principle with him, and one that I like to remember. "Never give a woman away, Bunny," he used to say; and he said it again to-night, but with a heavy cloud upon him, as though his chivalry was sorely tried.

"That's all right," said I, "if you're not going to be given away yourself."

"That's just it, Bunny! That's just—"

The words were out of him, it was too late to recall them. I had hit the nail upon the head.

"So she threatened you," I said, "did she?"

"I didn't say so," he replied, coldly.

"And she is mated with a clown!" I pursued.

"How she ever married him," he admitted, "is a mystery to me."

"It always is," said I, the wise man for once, and rather enjoying the role.

"Southern blood?"

"Spanish."

"She'll be pestering you to run off with her, old chap," said I.

Raffles was pacing the room. He stopped in his stride for half a second. So she had begun pestering him already! It is wonderful how acute any fool can be in the affairs of his friend.

But Raffles resumed his walk without a syllable, and I retreated to safer ground.

"So you sent her to Earl's Court," I mused aloud; and at last he smiled.

"You'll be interested to hear, Bunny," said he, "that I am now living in Seven Dials, and Bill Sikes couldn't hold a farthing dip to me. Bless you, she had my old police record at her fingers' ends, but it was fit to frame compared with the one I gave her. I had sunk as low as they dig. I divided my nights between the open parks and a thieves' kitchen in Seven Dials. If I was decently dressed it was because I had stolen the suit down the Thames Valley beat the night before last. I was on my way back when first that sleepy square, and then her open window, proved too much for me. You should have heard me beg her to let me push on to the devil in my own way; there I spread myself, for I meant every word; but I swore the final stage would be a six-foot drop."

"You did lay it on," said I.

"It was necessary, and that had its effect. She let me go. But at the last moment she said she didn't believe I was so black as I painted myself, and then there was the balcony scene you missed."

So that was all. I could not help telling him that he had got out of it better than he deserved for ever getting in. Next moment I regretted the remark.

"If I have got out of it," said Raffles, doubtfully. "We are dreadfully near neighbors, and I can't move in a minute, with old Theobald taking a grave view of my case. I suppose I had better lie low, and thank the gods again for putting her off the scent for the time being."

No doubt our conversation was carried beyond this point, but it certainly was not many minutes later, nor had we left the subject, when the electric bell thrilled us both to a sudden silence.

"The doctor?" I queried, hope fighting with my horror.

"It was a single ring."

"The last post?"

"You know he knocks, and it's long past his time."

The electric bell rang again, but now as though it never would stop.

"You go, Bunny," said Raffles, with decision. His eyes were sparkling. His smile was firm.

"What am I to say?"

"If it's the lady let her in."

It was the lady, still in her evening cloak, with her fine dark head half-hidden by the hood, and an engaging contempt of appearances upon her angry face. She was even handsomer than I had thought, and her beauty of a bolder type, but she was also angrier than I had anticipated when I came so readily to the door. The passage into which it opened was an exceedingly narrow one, as I have often said, but I never dreamt of barring this woman's way, though not a word did she stoop to say to me. I was only too glad to flatten myself against the wall, as the rustling fury strode past me into the lighted room with the open door.

"So this is your thieves' kitchen!" she cried, in high-pitched scorn.

I was on the threshold myself, and Raffles glanced towards me with raised eyebrows.

"I have certainly had better quarters in my day," said he, "but you need not call them absurd names before my man."

"Then send your 'man' about his business," said Jacques Saillard, with an unpleasant stress upon the word indicated.

But when the door was shut I heard Raffles assuring her that I knew nothing, that he was a real invalid overcome by a sudden mad temptation, and all he had told her of his life a lie to hide his whereabouts, but all he was telling her now she could prove for herself without leaving that building. It seemed, however, that she had proved it already by going first to the porter below stairs. Yet I do not think she cared one atom which story was the truth.

"So you thought I could pass you in your chair," she said, "or ever in this world again, without hearing from my heart that it was you!"

II

"Bunny," said Raffles, "I'm awfully sorry, old chap, but you've got to go."

It was some weeks since the first untimely visitation of Jacques Saillard, but there had been many others at all hours of the day, while Raffles had been induced to pay at least one to her studio in the neighboring square. These intrusions he had endured at first with an air of humorous resignation which imposed upon me less than he imagined. The woman meant well, he said, after all, and could be trusted to keep his secret loyally. It was plain to me, however, that Raffles did not trust her, and that his pretence upon the point was a deliberate pose to conceal the extent to which she had him in her power. Otherwise there would have been little point in hiding anything from the one person in possession of the cardinal secret of his identity.

But Raffles thought it worth his while to hoodwink Jacques Saillard in the subsidiary matter of his health, in which Dr. Theobald lent him unwitting assistance, and, as we have seen, to impress upon her that I was actually his attendant, and as ignorant of his past as the doctor himself. "So you're all right, Bunny," he had assured me; "she thinks you knew nothing the other night. I told you she wasn't a clever woman outside her work. But hasn't she a will!" I told Raffles it was very considerate of him to keep me out of it, but that it seemed to me like tying up the bag when the cat had escaped. His reply was an admission that one must be on the defensive with such a woman and in such a case. Soon after this, Raffles, looking far from well, fell back upon his own last line of defence, namely, his bed; and now, as always in the end, I could see some sense in his subtleties, since it was comparatively easy for me to turn even Jacques Saillard from the door, with Dr. Theobald's explicit injunctions, and with my own honesty unquestioned. So for a day we had peace once more. Then came letters, then the doctor again and again, and finally my dismissal in the incredible words which have necessitated these explanations.

"Go?" I echoed. "Go where?"

"It's that ass Theobald," said Raffles. "He insists."

"On my going altogether?"

He nodded.

"And you mean to let him have his way?"

I had no language for my mortification and disgust, though neither was as yet quite so great as my surprise. I had foreseen almost every conceivable consequence of the mad act which brought all this trouble to pass, but a voluntary division between Raffles and me had certainly never entered my calculations. Nor could I think that it had occurred to him before our egregious doctor's last visit, this very morning. Raffles had looked irritated as he broke the news to me from his pillow, and now there was some sympathy in the way he sat up in bed, as though he felt the thing himself.

"I am obliged to give in to the fellow," said he. "He's saving me from my friend, and I'm bound to humor him. But I can tell you that we've been arguing about you for the last half hour, Bunny. It was no use; the idiot has had his knife in you from the first; and he wouldn't see me through on any other conditions."

"So he is going to see you through, is he?"

"It tots up to that," said Raffles, looking at me rather hard. "At all events he has come to my rescue for the time being, and it's for me to manage the rest. You don't know what it has been, Bunny, these last few weeks; and gallantry forbids that I should tell you even now. But would you rather elope against your will, or have your continued existence made known to the world in general and the police in particular? That is practically the problem which I have had to solve, and the temporary solution was to fall ill. As a matter of fact, I am ill; and now what do you think? I owe it to you to tell you, Bunny, though it goes against the grain. She would take me 'to the dear, warm underworld, where the sun really shines,' and she would 'nurse me back to life and love!' The artistic temperament is a fearsome thing, Bunny, in a woman with the devil's own will!"

Raffles tore up the letter from which he had read these piquant extracts, and lay back on the pillows with the tired air of the veritable invalid which he seemed able to assume at will. But for once he did look as though bed was the best place for him; and I used the fact as an argument for my own retention in defiance of Dr. Theobald. The town was full of typhoid, I said, and certainly that autumnal scourge was in the air. Did he want me to leave him at the very moment when he might be sickening for a serious illness?

"You know I don't, my good fellow," said Raffles, wearily; "but Theobald does, and I can't afford to go against him now. Not that I really care what happens to me now that that woman knows I'm in the land of the living; she'll let it out, to a dead certainty, and at the best there'll be a hue and cry, which is the very thing I have escaped all these years. Now, what I want you to do is to go and take some quiet place somewhere, and then let me know, so that I may have a port in the storm when it breaks."

"Now you're talking!" I cried, recovering my spirits. "I thought you meant to go and drop a fellow altogether!"

"Exactly the sort of thing you would think," rejoined Raffles, with a contempt that was welcome enough after my late alarm. "No, my dear rabbit, what you've got to do is to make a new burrow for us both. Try down the Thames, in some quiet nook that a literary man would naturally select. I've often thought that more use might be made of a boat, while the family are at dinner, than there ever has been yet. If Raffles is to come to life, old chap, he shall go a-Raffling for all he's worth! There's something to be done with a bicycle, too. Try Ham Common or Roehampton, or some such sleepy hollow a trifle off the line; and say you're expecting your brother from the colonies."

Into this arrangement I entered without the slightest hesitation, for we had funds enough to carry it out on a comfortable scale, and Raffles placed a sufficient share at my disposal for the nonce. Moreover, I for one was only too glad to seek fresh fields and pastures new—a phrase which I determined to interpret literally in my choice of fresh surroundings. I was tired of our submerged life in the poky little flat, especially now that we had money enough for better things. I myself of late had dark dealings with the receivers, with the result that poor Lord Ernest Belville's successes were now indeed ours. Subsequent complications had been the more galling on that account, while the wanton way in which they had been created was the most irritating reflection of all. But it had brought its own punishment upon Raffles, and I fancied the lesson would prove salutary when we again settled down.

"If ever we do, Bunny!" said he, as I took his hand and told him how I was already looking forward to the time.

"But of course we will!" I cried, concealing the resentment at leaving him which his tone and his appearance renewed in my breast.

"I'm not so sure of it," he said, gloomily. "I'm in somebody's clutches, and I've got to get out of them first."

"I'll sit tight until you do."

"Well," he said, "if you don't see me in ten days you never will."

"Only ten days?" I echoed. "That's nothing at all."

"A lot may happen in ten days," replied Raffles, in the same depressing tone, so very depressing in him; and with that he held out his hand a second time, and dropped mine suddenly after as sudden a pressure for farewell.

I left the flat in considerable dejection after all, unable to decide whether Raffles was really ill, or only worried as I knew him to be. And at the foot of the stairs the author of my dismissal, that confounded Theobald, flung open his door and waylaid me.

"Are you going?" he demanded.

The traps in my hands proclaimed that I was, but I dropped them at his feet to have it out with him then and there.

"Yes," I answered fiercely, "thanks to you!"

"Well, my good fellow," he said, his full-blooded face lightening and softening at the same time, as though a load were off his mind, "it's no pleasure to me to deprive any man of his billet, but you never were a nurse, and you know that as well as I do."

I began to wonder what he meant, and how much he did know, and my speculations kept me silent. "But come in here a moment," he continued, just as I decided that he knew nothing at all. And, leading me into his minute consulting-room, Dr. Theobald solemnly presented me with a sovereign by way of compensation, which I pocketed as solemnly, and with as much gratitude as if I had not fifty of them distributed over my person as it was. The good fellow had quite forgotten my social status, about which he himself had been so particular at our earliest interview; but he had never accustomed himself to treat me as a gentleman, and I do not suppose he had been improving his memory by the tall tumbler which I saw him poke behind a photograph as we entered.

"There's one thing I should like to know before I go," said I, turning suddenly on the doctor's mat, "and that is whether Mr. Maturin is really ill or not!"

I meant, of course, at the present moment, but Dr. Theobald braced himself like a recruit at the drill-sergeant's voice.

"Of course he is," he snapped—"so ill as to need a nurse who can nurse, by way of a change."

With that his door shut in my face, and I had to go my way, in the dark as to whether he had mistaken my meaning, and was telling me a lie, or not.

But for my misgivings upon this point I might have extracted some very genuine enjoyment out of the next few days. I had decent clothes to my back, with money, as I say, in most of the pockets, and more freedom to spend it than was possible in the constant society of a man whose personal liberty depended on a universal supposition that he was dead. Raffles was as bold as ever, and I as fond of him, but whereas he would run any risk in a professional exploit, there were many innocent recreations still open to me which would have been sheer madness in him. He could not even watch a match, from the sixpenny seats, at Lord's cricket-ground, where the Gentlemen were every year in a worse way without him. He never travelled by rail, and dining out was a risk only to be run with some ulterior object in view. In fact, much as it had changed, Raffles could no longer show his face with perfect impunity in any quarter or at any hour. Moreover, after the lesson he had now learnt, I foresaw increased caution on his part in this respect. But I myself was under no such perpetual disadvantage, and, while what was good enough for Raffles was quite good enough for me so long as we were together, I saw no harm in profiting by the present opportunity of "doing my-self well."

Such were my reflections on the way to Richmond in a hansom cab. Richmond had struck us both as the best centre of operations in search of the suburban retreat which Raffles wanted, and by road, in a well-appointed, well-selected hansom, was certainly the most agreeable way of getting there. In a week or ten days Raffles was to write to me at the Richmond post-office, but for at least a week I should be "on my own." It was not an unpleasant sensation as I leant back in the comfortable hansom, and rather to one side, in order to have a good look at myself in the bevelled mirror that is almost as great an improvement in these vehicles as the rubber tires. Really I was not an ill-looking youth, if one may call one's self such at the age of thirty. I could lay no claim either to the striking cast of countenance or to the peculiar charm of expression which made the face of Raffles like no other in the world. But this very distinction was in itself a danger, for its impression was indelible, whereas I might still have been mistaken for a hundred other young fellows at large in London. Incredible as it may appear to the moralists, I had sustained no external hallmark by my term of imprisonment, and I am vain enough to believe that the evil which I did had not a separate existence in my face. This afternoon, indeed, I was struck by the purity of my fresh complexion, and rather depressed by the general innocence of the visage which peered into mine from the little mirror. My straw-colored moustache, grown in the flat after a protracted holiday, again preserved the most disappointing dimensions, and was still invisible in certain lights without wax. So far from discerning the desperate criminal who has "done time" once, and deserved it over and over again, the superior but superficial observer might have imagined that he detected a certain element of folly in my face.

At all events it was not the face to shut the doors of a first-class hotel against me, without accidental evidence of a more explicit kind, and it was with no little satisfaction that I directed the man to drive to the Star and Garter. I also told him to go through Richmond Park, though he warned me that it would add considerably to the distance and his fare. It was autumn, and it struck me that the tints would be fine. And I had learnt from Raffles to appreciate such things, even amid the excitement of an audacious enterprise.

If I dwell upon my appreciation of this occasion it is because, like most pleasures, it was exceedingly short-lived. I was very comfortable at the Star and Garter, which was so empty that I had a room worthy of a prince, where I could enjoy the finest of all views (in patriotic opinion) every morning while I shaved. I walked many miles through the noble park, over the commons of Ham and Wimbledon, and one day as far as that of Esher, where I was forcibly reminded of a service we once rendered to a distinguished resident in this delightful locality. But it was on Ham Common, one of the places which Raffles had mentioned as specially desirable, that I actually found an almost ideal retreat. This was a cottage where I heard, on inquiry, that rooms were to be let in the summer. The landlady, a motherly body, of visible excellence, was surprised indeed at receiving an application for the winter months; but I have generally found that the title of "author," claimed with an air, explains every little innocent irregularity of conduct or appearance, and even requires something of the kind to carry conviction to the lay intelligence. The present case was one in point, and when I said that I could only write in a room facing north, on mutton chops and milk, with a cold ham in the wardrobe in case of nocturnal inspiration, to which I was liable, my literary character was established beyond dispute. I secured the rooms, paid a month's rent in advance at my own request, and moped in them dreadfully until the week was up and Raffles due any day. I explained that the inspiration would not come, and asked abruptly if the mutton was New Zealand.

Thrice had I made fruitless inquiries at the Richmond post-office; but on the tenth day I was in and out almost every hour. Not a word was there for me up to the last post at night. Home I trudged to Ham with horrible forebodings, and back again to Richmond after breakfast next morning. Still there was nothing. I could bear it no more. At ten minutes to eleven I was climbing the station stairs at Earl's Court.

It was a wretched morning there, a weeping mist shrouding the long, straight street, and clinging to one's face in clammy caresses. I felt how much better it was down at Ham, as I turned into our side street, and saw the flats looming like mountains, the chimney-pots hidden in the mist. At our entrance stood a nebulous conveyance, that I took at first for a tradesman's van; to my horror it proved to be a hearse; and all at once the white breath ceased upon my lips.

I had looked up at our windows and the blinds were down!

I rushed within. The doctor's door stood open. I neither knocked nor rang, but found him in his consulting-room with red eyes and a blotchy face. Otherwise he was in solemn black from head to heel.

"Who is dead?" I burst out. "Who is dead?"

The red eyes looked redder than ever as Dr. Theobald opened them at the unwarrantable sight of me; and he was terribly slow in answering. But in the end he did answer, and did not kick me out as he evidently had a mind.

"Mr. Maturin," he said, and sighed like a beaten man.

I said nothing. It was no surprise to me. I had known it all these minutes. Nay, I had dreaded this from the first, had divined it at the last, though to the last also I had refused to entertain my own conviction. Raffles dead! A real invalid after all! Raffles dead, and on the point of burial!

"What did he die of?" I asked, unconsciously drawing on that fund of grim self-control which the weakest of us seem to hold in reserve for real calamity.

"Typhoid," he answered. "Kensington is full of it."

"He was sickening for it when I left, and you knew it, and could get rid of me then!"

"My good fellow, I was obliged to have a more experienced nurse for that very reason."

The doctor's tone was so conciliatory that I remembered in an instant what a humbug the man was, and became suddenly possessed with the vague conviction that he was imposing upon me now.

"Are you sure it was typhoid at all?" I cried fiercely to his face. "Are you sure it wasn't suicide—or murder?"

I confess that I can see little point in this speech as I write it down, but it was what I said in a burst of grief and of wild suspicion; nor was it without effect upon Dr. Theobald, who turned bright scarlet from his well-brushed hair to his immaculate collar.

"Do you want me to throw you out into the street?" he cried; and all at once I remembered that I had come to Raffles as a perfect stranger, and for his sake might as well preserve that character to the last.

"I beg your pardon," I said, brokenly. "He was so good to me—I became so attached to him. You forget I am originally of his class."

"I did forget it," replied Theobald, looking relieved at my new tone, "and I beg Your pardon for doing so. Hush! They are bringing him down. I must have a drink before we start, and you'd better join me."

There was no pretence about his drink this time, and a pretty stiff one it was, but I fancy my own must have run it hard. In my case it cast a merciful haze over much of the next hour, which I can truthfully describe as one of the most painful of my whole existence. I can have known very little of what I was doing. I only remember finding myself in a hansom, suddenly wondering why it was going so slowly, and once more awaking to the truth. But it was to the truth itself more than to the liquor that I must have owed my dazed condition. My next recollection is of looking down into the open grave, in a sudden passionate anxiety to see the name for myself. It was not the name of my friend, of course, but it was the one under which he had passed for many months.

I was still stupefied by a sense of inconceivable loss, and had not raised my eyes from that which was slowly forcing me to realize what had happened, when there was a rustle at my elbow, and a shower of hothouse flowers passed before them, falling like huge snowflakes where my gaze had rested. I looked up, and at my side stood a majestic figure in deep mourning. The face was carefully veiled, but I was too close not to recognize the masterful beauty whom the world knew as Jacques Saillard. I had no sympathy with her; on the contrary, my blood boiled with the vague conviction that in some way she was responsible for this death. Yet she was the only woman present—there were not a half a dozen of us altogether—and her flowers were the only flowers.

The melancholy ceremony was over, and Jacques Saillard had departed in a funeral brougham, evidently hired for the occasion. I had watched her drive away, and the sight of my own cabman, making signs to me through the fog, had suddenly reminded me that I had bidden him to wait. I was the last to leave, and had turned my back upon the grave-diggers, already at their final task, when a hand fell lightly but firmly upon my shoulder.

"I don't want to make a scene in a cemetery," said a voice, in a not unkindly, almost confidential whisper. "Will you get into your own cab and come quietly?"

"Who on earth are you?" I exclaimed.

I now remembered having seen the fellow hovering about during the funeral, and subconsciously taking him for the undertaker's head man. He had certainly that appearance, and even now I could scarcely believe that he was anything else.

"My name won't help you," he said, pityingly. "But you will guess where I come from when I tell you I have a warrant for your arrest."

My sensations at this announcement may not be believed, but I solemnly declare that I have seldom experienced so fierce a satisfaction. Here was a new excitement in which to drown my grief; here was something to think about; and I should be spared the intolerable experience of a solitary return to the little place at Ham. It was as though I had lost a limb and some one had struck me so hard in the face that the greater agony was forgotten. I got into the hansom without a word, my captor following at my heels, and giving his own directions

E.W. HORNUNG

to the cabman before taking his seat. The word "station" was the only one I caught, and I wondered whether it was to be Bow Street again. My companion's next words, however, or rather the tone in which he uttered them, destroyed my capacity for idle speculation.

"Mr. Maturin!" said he. "Mr. Maturin indeed!"

"Well," said I, "what about him?"

"Do you think we don't know who he was?"

"Who was he?" I asked, defiantly.

"You ought to know," said he. "You got locked up through him the other time, too. His favorite name was Raffles then."

"It was his real name," I said, indignantly. "And he has been dead for years."

My captor simply chuckled.

"He's at the bottom of the sea, I tell you!"

But I do not know why I should have told him with such spirit, for what could it matter to Raffles now? I did not think; instinct was still stronger than reason, and, fresh from his funeral, I had taken up the cudgels for my dead friend as though he were still alive. Next moment I saw this for myself, and my tears came nearer the surface than they had been yet; but the fellow at my side laughed outright.

"Shall I tell you something else?" said he.

"As you like."

"He's not even at the bottom of that grave! He's no more dead than you or I, and a sham burial is his latest piece of villainy!"

I doubt whether I could have spoken if I had tried. I did not try. I had no use for speech. I did not even ask him if he was sure, I was so sure myself. It was all as plain to me as riddles usually are when one has the answer. The doctor's alarms, his unscrupulous venality, the simulated illness, my own dismissal, each fitted in its obvious place, and not even the last had power as yet to mar my joy in the one central fact to which all the rest were as tapers to the sun.

"He is alive!" I cried. "Nothing else matters—he is alive!"

At last I did ask whether they had got him too; but thankful as I was for the greater knowledge, I confess that I did not much care what answer I received. Already I was figuring out how much we might each get, and how old we should be when we came out. But my companion tilted his hat to the back of his head, at the same time putting his face close to mine, and compelling my scrutiny. And my answer, as you have already guessed, was the face of Raffles himself, superbly disguised (but less superbly than his voice), and yet so thinly that I should have known him in a trice had I not been too miserable in the beginning to give him a second glance.

Jacques Saillard had made his life impossible, and this was the one escape. Raffles had bought the doctor for a thousand pounds, and the doctor had bought a "nurse" of his own kidney, on his own account; me, for some reason, he would not trust; he had insisted upon my dismissal as an essential preliminary to his part in the conspiracy. Here the details were half-humorous, half-grewsome, each in turn as Raffles told me the story. At one period he had been very daringly drugged indeed, and, in his own words, "as dead as a man need be"; but he had left strict instructions that nobody but the nurse and "my devoted physician" should "lay a finger on me" afterwards; and by virtue of this proviso a library of books (largely acquired for the occasion) had been impiously interred at Kensal Green. Raffles had definitely undertaken not to trust me with the secret, and, but for my untoward appearance at the funeral (which he had attended for his own final satisfaction), I was assured and am convinced that he would have kept his promise to the letter. In explaining this he gave me the one explanation I desired, and in another moment we turned into Praed Street, Paddington.

"And I thought you said Bow Street!" said I. "Are you coming straight down to Richmond with me?"

"I may as well," said Raffles, "though I did mean to get my kit first, so as to start in fair and square as the long-lost brother from the bush. That's why I hadn't written. The function was a day later than I calculated. I was going to write to-night."

"But what are we to do?" said I, hesitating when he had paid the cab. "I have been playing the colonies for all they are worth!"

"Oh, I've lost my luggage," said he, "or a wave came into my cabin and spoilt every stitch, or I had nothing fit to bring ashore. We'll settle that in the train."

The Wrong House

My brother Ralph, who now lived with me on the edge of Ham Common, had come home from Australia with a curious affection of the eyes, due to long exposure to the glare out there, and necessitating the use of clouded spectacles in the open air. He had not the rich complexion of the typical colonist, being indeed peculiarly pale, but it appeared that he had been confined to his berth for the greater part of the voyage, while his prematurely gray hair was sufficient proof that the rigors of bush life had at last undermined an originally tough constitution. Our landlady, who spoilt my brother from the first, was much concerned on his behalf, and wished to call in the local doctor; but Ralph said dreadful things about the profession, and quite frightened the good woman by arbitrarily forbidding her ever to let a doctor inside her door. I had to apologize to her for the painful prejudices and violent language of "these colonists," but the old soul was easily mollified. She had fallen in love with my brother at first sight, and she never could do too much for him. It was owing to our landlady that I took to calling him Ralph, for the first time in our lives, on her beginning to speak of and to him as "Mr. Raffles."

"This won't do," said he to me. "It's a name that sticks."

"It must be my fault! She must have heard it from me," said I self-reproachfully.

"You must tell her it's the short for Ralph."

"But it's longer."

"It's the short," said he; "and you've got to tell her so."

Henceforth I heard as much of "Mr. Ralph," his likes and dislikes, what he would fancy and what he would not, and oh, what a dear gentleman he was, that I often remembered to say "Ralph, old chap," myself.

It was an ideal cottage, as I said when I found it, and in it our delicate man became rapidly robust. Not that the air was also ideal, for, when it was not raining, we had the same faithful mist from November to March. But it was something to Ralph to get any air at all, other than night-air, and the bicycle did the rest. We taught ourselves, and may I never forget our earlier rides, through and through Richmond Park when the afternoons were shortest, upon the incomparable Ripley Road when we gave a day to it. Raffles rode a Beeston Humber, a Royal

Sunbeam was good enough for me, but he insisted on our both having Dunlop tires.

"They seem the most popular brand. I had my eye on the road all the way from Ripley to Cobham, and there were more Dunlop marks than any other kind. Bless you, yes, they all leave their special tracks, and we don't want ours to be extra special; the Dunlop's like a rattlesnake, and the Palmer leaves telegraph-wires, but surely the serpent is more in our line."

That was the winter when there were so many burglaries in the Thames Valley from Richmond upward. It was said that the thieves used bicycles in every case, but what is not said? They were sometimes on foot to my knowledge, and we took a great interest in the series, or rather sequence of successful crimes. Raffles would often get his devoted old lady to read him the latest local accounts, while I was busy with my writing (much I wrote) in my own room. We even rode out by night ourselves, to see if we could not get on the tracks of the thieves, and never did we fail to find hot coffee on the hob for our return. We had indeed fallen upon our feet. Also, the misty nights might have been made for the thieves. But their success was not so consistent, and never so enormous as people said, especially the sufferers, who lost more valuables than they had ever been known to possess. Failure was often the caitiff's portion, and disaster once; owing, ironically enough, to that very mist which should have served them. But as I am going to tell the story with some particularity, and perhaps some gusto, you will see why who read.

The right house stood on high ground near the river, with quite a drive (in at one gate and out at the other) sweeping past the steps. Between the two gates was a half-moon of shrubs, to the left of the steps a conservatory, and to their right the walk leading to the tradesmen's entrance and the back premises; here also was the pantry window, of which more anon. The right house was the residence of an opulent stockbroker who wore a heavy watch-chain and seemed fair game. There would have been two objections to it had I been the stockbroker. The house was one of a row, though a goodly row, and an army-crammer had established himself next door. There is a type of such institutions in the suburbs; the youths go about in knickerbockers, smoking pipes, except on Saturday nights, when they lead each other home from the last train. It was none of our business to spy upon these boys, but their manners and customs fell within the field of observation.

And we did not choose the night upon which the whole row was likely to be kept awake.

The night that we did choose was as misty as even the Thames Valley is capable of making them. Raffles smeared vaseline upon the plated parts of his Beeston Humber before starting, and our dear landlady cosseted us both, and prayed we might see nothing of the nasty burglars, not denying as the reward would be very handy to them that got it, to say nothing of the honor and glory. We had promised her a liberal perquisite in the event of our success, but she must not give other cyclists our idea by mentioning it to a soul. It was about midnight when we cycled through Kingston to Surbiton, having trundled our machines across Ham Fields, mournful in the mist as those by Acheron, and so over Teddington Bridge.

I often wonder why the pantry window is the vulnerable point of nine houses out of ten. This house of ours was almost the tenth, for the window in question had bars of sorts, but not the right sort. The only bars that Raffles allowed to beat him were the kind that are let into the stone outside; those fixed within are merely screwed to the woodwork, and you can unscrew as many as necessary if you take the trouble and have the time. Barred windows are usually devoid of other fasteners worthy the name; this one was no exception to that foolish rule, and a push with the pen-knife did its business. I am giving householders some valuable hints, and perhaps deserving a good mark from the critics. These, in any case, are the points that I would see to, were I a rich stockbroker in a riverside suburb. In giving good advice, however, I should not have omitted to say that we had left our machines in the semi-circular shrubbery in front, or that Raffles had most ingeniously fitted our lamps with dark slides, which enabled us to leave them burning.

It proved sufficient to unscrew the bars at the bottom only, and then to wrench them to either side. Neither of us had grown stout with advancing years, and in a few minutes we both had wormed through into the sink, and thence to the floor. It was not an absolutely noiseless process, but once in the pantry we were mice, and no longer blind mice. There was a gas-bracket, but we did not meddle with that. Raffles went armed these nights with a better light than gas; if it were not immoral, I might recommend a dark-lantern which was more or less his patent. It was that handy invention, the electric torch, fitted by Raffles with a dark hood to fulfil the functions of a slide. I had held it through the bars while he undid the screws, and now he held it to the keyhole, in which a key was turned upon the other side.

There was a pause for consideration, and in the pause we put on our masks. It was never known that these Thames Valley robberies were all committed by miscreants decked in the livery of crime, but that was because until this night we had never even shown our masks. It was a point upon which Raffles had insisted on all feasible occasions since his furtive return to the world. To-night it twice nearly lost us everything—but you shall hear.

There is a forceps for turning keys from the wrong side of the door, but the implement is not so easy of manipulation as it might be. Raffles for one preferred a sharp knife and the corner of the panel. You go through the panel because that is thinnest, of course in the corner nearest the key, and you use a knife when you can, because it makes least noise. But it does take minutes, and even I can remember shifting the electric torch from one hand to the other before the aperture was large enough to receive the hand and wrist of Raffles.

He had at such times a motto of which I might have made earlier use, but the fact is that I have only once before described a downright burglary in which I assisted, and that without knowing it at the time. The most solemn student of these annals cannot affirm that he has cut through many doors in our company, since (what was to me) the maiden effort to which I allude. I, however, have cracked only too many a crib in conjunction with A. J. Raffles, and at the crucial moment he would whisper "Victory or Wormwood Scrubs, Bunny!" or instead of Wormwood Scrubs it might be Portland Bill. This time it was neither one nor the other, for with that very word "victory" upon his lips, they whitened and parted with the first taste of defeat.

"My hand's held!" gasped Raffles, and the white of his eyes showed all round the iris, a rarer thing than you may think.

At the same moment I heard the shuffling feet and the low, excited young voices on the other side of the door, and a faint light shone round Raffles's wrist.

"Well done, Beefy!"

"Hang on to him!"

"Good old Beefy!"

"Beefy's got him!"

"So have I—so have I!"

And Raffles caught my arm with his one free hand. "They've got me tight," he whispered. "I'm done."

"Blaze through the door," I urged, and might have done it had I been armed. But I never was. It was Raffles who monopolized that risk.

"I can't—it's the boys—the wrong house!" he whispered. "Curse the fog—it's done me. But you get out, Bunn, while you can; never mind me; it's my turn, old chap."

His one hand tightened in affectionate farewell. I put the electric torch in it before I went, trembling in every inch, but without a word.

Get out! His turn! Yes, I would get out, but only to come in again, for it was my turn—mine—not his. Would Raffles leave me held by a hand through a hole in a door? What he would have done in my place was the thing for me to do now. I began by diving head-first through the pantry window and coming to earth upon all fours. But even as I stood up, and brushed the gravel from the palms of my hands and the knees of my knickerbockers, I had no notion what to do next. And yet I was halfway to the front door before I remembered the vile crape mask upon my face, and tore it off as the door flew open and my feet were on the steps.

"He's into the next garden," I cried to a bevy of pyjamas with bare feet and young faces at either end of them.

"Who? Who?" said they, giving way before me.

"Some fellow who came through one of your windows head-first."

"The other Johnny, the other Johnny," the cherubs chorused.

"Biking past—saw the light—why, what have you there?"

Of course it was Raffles's hand that they had, but now I was in the hall among them. A red-faced barrel of a boy did all the holding, one hand round the wrist, the other palm to palm, and his knees braced up against the panel. Another was rendering ostentatious but ineffectual aid, and three or four others danced about in their pyjamas. After all, they were not more than four to one. I had raised my voice, so that Raffles might hear me and take heart, and now I raised it again. Yet to this day I cannot account for my inspiration, that proved nothing less.

"Don't talk so loud," they were crying below their breath; "don't wake 'em upstairs, this is our show."

"Then I see you've got one of them," said I, as desired. "Well, if you want the other you can have him, too. I believe he's hurt himself."

"After him, after him!" they exclaimed as one.

"But I think he got over the wall—"

"Come on, you chaps, come on!"

And there was a soft stampede to the hall door.

"Don't all desert me, I say!" gasped the red-faced hero who held Raffles prisoner.

"We must have them both, Beefy!"

"That's all very well—"

"Look here," I interposed, "I'll stay by you. I've a friend outside, I'll get him too."

"Thanks awfully," said the valiant Beefy.

The hall was empty now. My heart beat high.

"How did you hear them?" I inquired, my eye running over him.

"We were down having drinks—game o' Nap—in there."

Beefy jerked his great head toward an open door, and the tail of my eye caught the glint of glasses in the firelight, but the rest of it was otherwise engaged.

"Let me relieve you," I said, trembling.

"No, I'm all right."

"Then I must insist."

And before he could answer I had him round the neck with such a will that not a gurgle passed my fingers, for they were almost buried in his hot, smooth flesh. Oh, I am not proud of it; the act was as vile as act could be; but I was not going to see Raffles taken, my one desire was to be the saving of him, and I tremble even now to think to what lengths I might have gone for its fulfilment. As it was, I squeezed and tugged until one strong hand gave way after the other and came feeling round for me, but feebly because they had held on so long. And what do you suppose was happening at the same moment? The pinched white hand of Raffles, reddening with returning blood, and with a clot of blood upon the wrist, was craning upward and turning the key in the lock without a moment's loss.

"Steady on, Bunny!"

And I saw that Beefy's ears were blue; but Raffles was feeling in his pockets as he spoke. "Now let him breathe," said he, clapping his handkerchief over the poor youth's mouth. An empty vial was in his other hand, and the first few stertorous breaths that the poor boy took were the end of him for the time being. Oh, but it was villainous, my part especially, for he must have been far gone to go the rest of the way so readily. I began by saying I was not proud of this deed, but its dastardly character has come home to me more than ever with the penance of writing it out. I see in myself, at least my then self, things that I never saw quite so clearly before. Yet let me be quite sure that I would not do the same again. I had not the smallest desire to throttle this innocent lad (nor did I), but only to extricate Raffles from the most hopeless position he was ever in; and after all it was better than a blow from behind. On the whole, I will not alter a word, nor whine about the thing any more.

We lifted the plucky fellow into Raffles's place in the pantry, locked the door on him, and put the key through the panel. Now was the moment for thinking of ourselves, and again that infernal mask which Raffles swore by came near the undoing of us both. We had reached the steps when we were hailed by a voice, not from without but from within, and I had just time to tear the accursed thing from Raffles's face before he turned.

A stout man with a blonde moustache was on the stairs, in his pyjamas like the boys.

"What are you doing here?" said he.

"There has been an attempt upon your house," said I, still spokesman for the night, and still on the wings of inspiration.

"Your sons—"

"My pupils."

"Indeed. Well, they heard it, drove off the thieves, and have given chase."

"And where do you come in?" inquired the stout man, descending.

"We were bicycling past, and I actually saw one fellow come head-first through your pantry window. I think he got over the wall."

Here a breathless boy returned.

"Can't see anything of him," he gasped.

"It's true, then," remarked the crammer.

"Look at that door," said I.

But unfortunately the breathless boy looked also, and now he was being joined by others equally short of wind.

"Where's Beefy?" he screamed. "What on earth's happened to Beefy?"

"My good boys," exclaimed the crammer, "will one of you be kind enough to tell me what you've been doing, and what these gentlemen have been doing for you? Come in all, before you get your death. I see lights in the class-room, and more than lights. Can these be signs of a carouse?"

"A very innocent one, sir," said a well set-up youth with more moustache than I have yet.

"Well, Olphert, boys will be boys. Suppose you tell me what happened, before we come to recriminations."

The bad old proverb was my first warning. I caught two of the youths exchanging glances under raised eyebrows. Yet their stout, easy-going mentor had given me such a reassuring glance of side-long humor, as between man of the world and man of the world, that it was difficult to suspect him of suspicion. I was nevertheless itching to be gone.

Young Olphert told his story with engaging candor. It was true that they had come down for an hour's Nap and cigarettes; well, and there was no denying that there was whiskey in the glasses. The boys were now all back in their class-room, I think entirely for the sake of warmth; but Raffles and I were in knickerbockers and Norfolk jackets, and very naturally remained without, while the army-crammer (who wore bedroom slippers) stood on the threshold, with an eye each way. The more I saw of the man the better I liked and the more I feared him. His chief annoyance thus far was that they had not called him when they heard the noise, that they had dreamt of leaving him out of the fun. But he seemed more hurt than angry about that.

"Well, sir," concluded Olphert, "we left old Beefy Smith hanging on to his hand, and this gentleman with him, so perhaps he can tell us what happened next?"

"I wish I could," I cried with all their eyes upon me, for I had had time to think. "Some of you must have heard me say I'd fetch my friend in from the road?"

"Yes, I did," piped an innocent from within.

"Well, and when I came back with him things were exactly as you see them now. Evidently the man's strength was too much for the boy's; but whether he ran upstairs or outside I know no more than you do."

"It wasn't like that boy to run either way," said the crammer, cocking a clear blue eye on me.

"But if he gave chase!"

"It wasn't like him even to let go."

"I don't believe Beefy ever would," put in Olphert. "That's why we gave him the billet."

"He may have followed him through the pantry window," I suggested wildly.

E.W. HORNUNG

"But the door's shut," put in a boy.

"I'll have a look at it," said the crammer.

And the key no longer in the lock, and the insensible youth within! The key would be missed, the door kicked in; nay, with the man's eye still upon me, I thought I could smell the chloroform.

I thought I could hear a moan, and prepared for either any moment. And how he did stare! I have detested blue eyes ever since, and blonde moustaches, and the whole stout easy-going type that is not such a fool as it looks. I had brazened it out with the boys, but the first grown man was too many for me, and the blood ran out of my heart as though there was no Raffles at my back. Indeed, I had forgotten him. I had so longed to put this thing through by myself! Even in my extremity it was almost a disappointment to me when his dear, cool voice fell like a delicious draught upon my ears. But its effect upon the others is more interesting to recall. Until now the crammer had the centre of the stage, but at this point Raffles usurped a place which was always his at will. People would wait for what he had to say, as these people waited now for the simplest and most natural thing in the world.

"One moment!" he had begun.

"Well?" said the crammer, relieving me of his eyes at last.

"I don't want to lose any of the fun—"

"Nor must you," said the crammer, with emphasis.

"But we've left our bikes outside, and mine's a Beeston Humber," continued Raffles. "If you don't mind, we'll bring 'em in before these fellows get away on them."

And out he went without a look to see the effect of his words, I after him with a determined imitation of his self-control. But I would have given something to turn round. I believe that for one moment the shrewd instructor was taken in, but as I reached the steps I heard him asking his pupils whether any of them had seen any bicycles outside.

That moment, however, made the difference. We were in the shrubbery, Raffles with his electric torch drawn and blazing, when we heard the kicking at the pantry door, and in the drive with our bicycles before man and boys poured pell-mell down the steps.

We rushed our machines to the nearer gate, for both were shut, and we got through and swung it home behind us in the nick of time. Even I could mount before they could reopen the gate, which Raffles held against them for half an instant with unnecessary gallantry. But he would see me in front of him, and so it fell to me to lead the way.

Now, I have said that it was a very misty night (hence the whole thing), and also that these houses were on a hill. But they were not nearly on the top of the hill, and I did what I firmly believe that almost everybody would have done in my place. Raffles, indeed, said he would have done it himself, but that was his generosity, and he was the one man who would not. What I did was to turn in the opposite direction to the other gate, where we might so easily have been cut off, and to pedal for my life—up-hill!

"My God!" I shouted when I found it out.

"Can you turn in your own length?" asked Raffles, following loyally.

"Not certain."

"Then stick to it. You couldn't help it. But it's the devil of a hill!"

"And here they come!"

"Let them," said Raffles, and brandished his electric torch, our only light as yet.

A hill seems endless in the dark, for you cannot see the end, and with the patter of bare feet gaining on us, I thought this one could have no end at all. Of course the boys could charge up it quicker than we could pedal, but I even heard the voice of their stout instructor growing louder through the mist.

"Oh, to think I've let you in for this!" I groaned, my head over the handle-bars, every ounce of my weight first on one foot and then on the other. I glanced at Raffles, and in the white light of his torch he was doing it all with his ankles, exactly as though he had been riding in a Gymkhana.

"It's the most sporting chase I was ever in," said he.

"All my fault!"

"My dear Bunny, I wouldn't have missed it for the world!"

Nor would he forge ahead of me, though he could have done so in a moment, he who from his boyhood had done everything of the kind so much better than anybody else. No, he must ride a wheel's length behind me, and now we could not only hear the boys running, but breathing also. And then of a sudden I saw Raffles on my right striking with his torch; a face flew out of the darkness to meet the thick glass bulb with the glowing wire enclosed; it was the face of the boy Olphert, with his enviable moustache, but it vanished with the crash of glass, and the naked wire thickened to the eye like a tuning-fork struck red-hot.

I saw no more of that. One of them had crept up on my side also; as I looked, hearing him pant, he was grabbing at my left handle, and I nearly sent Raffles into the hedge by the sharp turn I took to the right. His wheel's length saved him. But my boy could run, was overhauling me again, seemed certain of me this time, when all at once the Sunbeam ran easily; every ounce of my weight with either foot once more, and I was over the crest of the hill, the gray road reeling out from under me as I felt for my brake. I looked back at Raffles. He had put up his feet. I screwed my head round still further, and there were the boys in their pyjamas, their hands upon their knees, like so many wicket-keepers, and a big man shaking his fist. There was a lamp-post on the hill-top, and that was the last I saw.

We sailed down to the river, then on through Thames Ditton as far as Esher Station, when we turned sharp to the right, and from the dark stretch by Imber Court came to light in Molesey, and were soon pedalling like gentlemen of leisure through Bushey Park, our lights turned up, the broken torch put out and away. The big gates had long been shut, but you can manoeuvre a bicycle through the others. We had no further adventures on the way home, and our coffee was still warm upon the hob.

"But I think it's an occasion for Sullivans," said Raffles, who now kept them for such. "By all my gods, Bunny, it's been the most sporting night we ever had in our lives! And do you know which was the most sporting part of it?"

"That up-hill ride?"

"I wasn't thinking of it."

"Turning your torch into a truncheon?"

"My dear Bunny! A gallant lad—I hated hitting him."

"I know," I said. "The way you got us out of the house!"

"No, Bunny," said Raffles, blowing rings. "It came before that, you sinner, and you know it!"

"You don't mean anything I did?" said I, self-consciously, for I began to see that this was what he did mean. And now at latest it will also be seen why this story has been told with undue and inexcusable gusto; there is none other like it for me to tell; it is my one ewe-lamb in all these annals. But Raffles had a ruder name for it.

"It was the Apotheosis of the Bunny," said he, but in a tone I never shall forget.

"I hardly knew what I was doing or saying," I said. "The whole thing was a fluke."

"Then," said Raffles, "it was the kind of fluke I always trusted you to make when runs were wanted."

And he held out his dear old hand.

The Knees of the Gods

I

"The worst of this war," said Raffles, "is the way it puts a fellow off his work."

It was, of course, the winter before last, and we had done nothing dreadful since the early autumn. Undoubtedly the war was the cause. Not that we were among the earlier victims of the fever. I took disgracefully little interest in the Negotiations, while the Ultimatum appealed to Raffles as a sporting flutter. Then we gave the whole thing till Christmas. We still missed the cricket in the papers. But one russet afternoon we were in Richmond, and a terrible type was shouting himself hoarse with "'Eavy British lorsses—orful slorter o' the Bo-wers! Orful slorter! Orful slorter! 'Eavy British lorsses!" I thought the terrible type had invented it, but Raffles gave him more than he asked, and then I held the bicycle while he tried to pronounce Eland's Laagte. We were never again without our sheaf of evening papers, and Raffles ordered three morning ones, and I gave up mine in spite of its literary page. We became strategists. We knew exactly what Buller was to do on landing, and, still better, what the other Generals should have done. Our map was the best that could be bought, with flags that deserved a better fate than standing still. Raffles woke me to hear "The Absent-Minded Beggar" on the morning it appeared; he was one of the first substantial subscribers to the fund. By this time our dear landlady was more excited than we. To our enthusiasm for Thomas she added a personal bitterness against the Wild Boars, as she persisted in calling them, each time as though it were the first. I could linger over our landlady's attitude in the whole matter. That was her only joke about it, and the true humorist never smiled at it herself. But you had only to say a syllable for a venerable gentleman, declared by her to be at the bottom of it all, to hear what she could do to him if she caught him. She could put him in a cage and go on tour with him, and make him howl and dance for his food like a debased bear before a fresh audience every day. Yet a more kind-hearted woman I have never known. The war did not uplift our landlady as it did her lodgers.

But presently it ceased to have that precise effect upon us. Bad was being made worse and worse; and then came more than Englishmen could endure in that black week across which the names of three African villages are written forever in letters of blood. "All three pegs," groaned Raffles on the last morning of the week; "neck-and-crop, neck-and-crop!" It was his first word of cricket since the beginning of the war.

We were both depressed. Old school-fellows had fallen, and I know Raffles envied them; he spoke so wistfully of such an end. To cheer him up I proposed to break into one of the many more or less royal residences in our neighborhood; a tough crib was what he needed; but I will not trouble you with what he said to me. There was less crime in England that winter than for years past; there was none at all in Raffles. And yet there were those who could denounce the war!

So we went on for a few of those dark days, Raffles very glum and grim, till one fine morning the Yeomanry idea put new heart into us all. It struck me at once as the glorious scheme it was to prove, but it did not hit me where it hit others. I was not a fox-hunter, and the gentlemen of England would scarcely have owned me as one of them. The case of Raffles was in that respect still more hopeless (he who had even played for them at Lord's), and he seemed to feel it. He would not speak to me all the morning; in the afternoon he went for a walk alone. It was another man who came home, flourishing a small bottle packed in white paper.

"Bunny," said he, "I never did lift my elbow; it's the one vice I never had. It has taken me all these years to find my tipple, Bunny; but here it is, my panacea, my elixir, my magic philtre!"

I thought he had been at it on the road, and asked him the name of the stuff.

"Look and see, Bunny."

And if it wasn't a bottle of ladies' hair-dye, warranted to change any shade into the once fashionable yellow within a given number of applications!

"What on earth," said I, "are you going to do with this?"

"Dye for my country," he cried, swelling. "Dulce et decorum est, Bunny, my boy!"

"Do you mean that you are going to the front?"

"If I can without coming to it."

I looked at him as he stood in the firelight, straight as a dart, spare but wiry, alert, laughing, flushed from his wintry walk; and as I looked, all the years that I had known him, and more besides, slipped from him in my eyes. I saw him captain of the eleven at school. I saw him running with the muddy ball on days like this, running round the other fifteen as a sheep-dog round a flock of sheep. He had his cap on still, and but for the gray hairs underneath—but here I lost him in a sudden mist. It was not sorrow at his going, for I did not mean to let him go alone. It was enthusiasm, admiration, affection, and also, I believe, a sudden regret that he had not always appealed to that part of my nature to which he was appealing now. It was a little thrill of penitence. Enough of it.

"I think it great of you," I said, and at first that was all.

How he laughed at me. He had had his innings; there was no better way of getting out. He had scored off an African millionaire, the Players, a Queensland Legislator, the Camorra, the late Lord Ernest Belville, and again and again off Scotland Yard. What more could one man do in one lifetime? And at the worst it was the death to die: no bed, no doctor, no temperature—and Raffles stopped himself.

"No pinioning, no white cap," he added, "if you like that better."

"I don't like any of it," I cried, cordially; "you've simply got to come back."

"To what?" he asked, a strange look on him.

And I wondered—for one instant—whether my little thrill had gone through him. He was not a man of little thrills.

Then for a minute I was in misery. Of course I wanted to go too—he shook my hand without a word—but how could I? They would never have me, a branded jailbird, in the Imperial Yeomanry! Raffles burst out laughing; he had been looking very hard at me for about three seconds.

"You rabbit," he cried, "even to think of it! We might as well offer ourselves to the Metropolitan Police Force. No, Bunny, we go out to the Cape on our own, and that's where we enlist. One of these regiments of irregular horse is the thing for us; you spent part of your pretty penny on horse-flesh, I believe, and you remember how I rode in the bush! We're the very men for them, Bunny, and they won't ask to see our birthmarks out there. I don't think even my hoary locks would put them off, but it would be too conspicuous in the ranks."

Our landlady first wept on hearing our determination, and then longed to have the pulling of certain whiskers (with the tongs, and they should be red-hot); but from that day, and for as many as were left to us, the good soul made more of us than ever. Not that she was at all surprised; dear brave gentlemen who could look for burglars on their bicycles at dead of night, it was only what you might expect of them, bless their lion hearts. I wanted to wink at Raffles, but he would not catch my eye. He was a ginger-headed Raffles by the end of January, and it was extraordinary what a difference it made. His most elaborate disguises had not been more effectual than this simple expedient, and, with khaki to complete the subdual of his individuality, he had every hope of escaping recognition in the field. The man he dreaded was the officer he had known in old days; there were ever so many of him at the Front; and it was to minimize this risk that we went out second-class at the beginning of February.

It was a weeping day, a day in a shroud, cold as clay, yet for that very reason an ideal day upon which to leave England for the sunny Front. Yet my heart was heavy as I looked my last at her; it was heavy as the raw, thick air, until Raffles came and leant upon the rail at my side.

"I know what you are thinking, and you've got to stop," said he. "It's on the knees of the gods, Bunny, whether we do or we don't, and thinking won't make us see over their shoulders."

II

Now I MADE AS BAD a soldier (except at heart) as Raffles made a good one, and I could not say a harder thing of myself. My ignorance of matters military was up to that time unfathomable, and is still profound. I was always a fool with horses, though I did not think so at one time, and I had never been any good with a gun. The average Tommy may be my intellectual inferior, but he must know some part of his work better than I ever knew any of mine. I never even learnt to be killed. I do not mean that I ever ran away. The South African Field Force might have been strengthened if I had.

The foregoing remarks do not express a pose affected out of superiority to the usual spirit of the conquering hero, for no man was keener on the war than I, before I went to it. But one can only write with gusto of events (like that little affair at Surbiton) in which one has acquitted oneself without discredit, and I cannot say that of my part in the war, of which I now loathe the thought for other reasons. The battlefield was no place for me, and neither was the camp. My ineptitude made me the butt of the looting, cursing, swash-buckling lot who formed the very irregular squadron which we joined; and it would have gone hard with me but for Raffles, who was soon the darling devil of them all, but never more loyally my friend. Your fireside fire-eater does not think of these things. He imagines all the fighting to be with the enemy. He will probably be horrified to hear that men can detest each other as cordially in khaki as in any other wear, and with a virulence seldom inspired by the bearded dead-shot in the opposite trench. To the fireside fire-eater, therefore (for you have seen me one myself), I dedicate the story of Corporal Connal, Captain Bellingham, the General, Raffles, and myself.

I must be vague, for obvious reasons. The troop is fighting as I write; you will soon hear why I am not; but neither is Raffles, nor Corporal Connal. They are fighting as well as ever, those other hard-living, harder-dying sons of all soils; but I am not going to say where it was that we fought with them. I believe that no body of men of equal size has done half so much heroic work. But they had got themselves a bad name off the field, so to speak; and I am not going to make it worse by saddling them before the world with Raffles and myself, and that ruffian Connal.

The fellow was a mongrel type, a Glasgow Irishman by birth and upbringing, but he had been in South Africa for years, and he certainly knew the country very well. This circumstance, coupled with the fact that he was a very handy man with horses, as all colonists are, had procured him the first small step from the ranks which facilitates bullying if a man be a bully by nature, and is physically fitted to be a successful one. Connal was a hulking ruffian, and in me had ideal game. The brute was offensive to me from the hour I joined. The details are of no importance, but I stood up to him at first in words, and finally for a few seconds on my feet. Then I went down like an ox, and Raffles came out of his tent. Their fight lasted twenty minutes, and Raffles was marked, but the net result was dreadfully conventional, for the bully was a bully no more.

But I began gradually to suspect that he was something worse. All this time we were fighting every day, or so it seems when I look back. Never a great engagement, and yet never a day when we were wholly out of touch with the enemy. I had thus several opportunities of watching the other enemy under fire, and had almost convinced myself of the systematic harmlessness of his own shooting, when a more glaring incident occurred.

One night three troops of our squadron were ordered to a certain point whither they had patrolled the previous week; but our own particular troop was to stay behind, and in charge of no other than the villanous corporal, both our officer and sergeant having gone into hospital with enteric. Our detention, however, was very temporary, and Connal would seem to have received the usual vague orders to proceed in the early morning to the place where the other three companies had camped. It appeared that we were to form an escort to two squadron-wagons containing kits, provisions, and ammunition.

Before daylight Connal had reported his departure to the commanding officer, and we passed the outposts at gray dawn. Now, though I was perhaps the least observant person in the troop, I was not the least wideawake where Corporal Connal was concerned, and it struck me at once that we were heading in the wrong direction. My reasons are not material, but as a matter of fact our last week's patrol had pushed its khaki tentacles both east and west; and eastward they had met with resistance so determined as to compel them to retire; yet it was eastward that we were travelling now. I at once spurred alongside Raffles, as he rode, bronzed and bearded, with warworn wide-awake over eyes grown keen as a hawk's, and a cutty-pipe sticking straight out from his front teeth. I can see him now, so gaunt and grim and debonair, yet already with much of the nonsense gone out of him, though I thought he only smiled on my misgivings.

"Did he get the instructions, Bunny, or did we? Very well, then; give the devil a chance."

There was nothing further to be said, but I felt more crushed than convinced; so we jogged along into broad daylight, until Raffles himself gave a whistle of surprise.

"A white flag, Bunny, by all my gods!"

I could not see it; he had the longest sight in all our squadron; but in a little the fluttering emblem, which had gained such a sinister significance in most of our eyes, was patent even to mine. A little longer, and the shaggy Boer was in our midst upon his shaggy pony, with a half-scared, half-incredulous look in his deep-set eyes. He was on his way to our lines with some missive, and had little enough to say to us, though frivolous and flippant questions were showered upon him from most saddles.

"Any Boers over there?" asked one, pointing in the direction in which we were still heading.

"Shut up!" interjected Raffles in crisp rebuke.

The Boer looked stolid but sinister.

"Any of our chaps?" added another.

The Boer rode on with an open grin.

And the incredible conclusion of the matter was that we were actually within their lines in another hour; saw them as large as life within a mile and a half on either side of us; and must every man of us have been taken prisoner had not every man but Connal refused to go one inch further, and had not the Boers themselves obviously suspected some subtle ruse as the only conceivable explanation of so madcap a manoeuvre. They allowed us to retire without firing a shot; and retire you may be sure we did, the Kaffirs flogging their teams in a fury of fear, and our precious corporal sullen but defiant.

I have said this was the conclusion of the matter, and I blush to repeat that it practically was. Connal was indeed wheeled up before the colonel, but his instructions were not written instructions, and he lied his way out with equal hardihood and tact.

"You said 'over there,' sir," he stoutly reiterated; and the vagueness with which such orders were undoubtedly given was the saving of him for the time being.

I need not tell you how indignant I felt, for one.

"The fellow is a spy!" I said to Raffles, with no nursery oath, as we strolled within the lines that night.

He merely smiled in my face.

"And have you only just found it out, Bunny? I have known it almost ever since we joined; but this morning I did think we had him on toast."

"It's disgraceful that we had not," cried I. "He ought to have been shot like a dog."

"Not so loud, Bunny, though I quite agree; but I don't regret what has happened as much as you do. Not that I am less bloodthirsty than you are in this case, but a good deal more so! Bunny, I'm mad-keen on bowling him out with my own unaided hand—though I may ask you to take the wicket. Meanwhile, don't wear all your animosity upon your sleeve; the fellow has friends who still believe in him; and there is no need for you to be more openly his enemy than you were before."

Well, I can only vow that I did my best to follow this sound advice; but who but a Raffles can control his every look? It was never my forte, as you know, yet to this day I cannot conceive what I did to excite the treacherous corporal's suspicions. He was clever enough, however, not to betray them, and lucky enough to turn the tables on us, as you shall hear.

III

Bloemfontein had fallen since our arrival, but there was plenty of fight in the Free Staters still, and I will not deny that it was these gentry who were showing us the sport for which our corps came in. Constant skirmishing was our portion, with now and then an action that you would know at least by name, did I feel free to mention them. But I do not, and indeed it is better so. I have not to describe the war even as I saw it, I am thankful to say, but only the martial story of us two and those others of whom you wot. Corporal Connal was the dangerous blackguard you have seen. Captain Bellingham is best known for his position in the batting averages a year or two ago, and for his subsequent failure to obtain a place in any of the five Test Matches. But I only think of him as the officer who recognized Raffles.

We had taken a village, making quite a little name for it and for ourselves, and in the village our division was reinforced by a fresh brigade of the Imperial troops. It was a day of rest, our first for weeks, but Raffles and I spent no small part of it in seeking high and low for a worthy means of quenching the kind of thirst which used to beset Yeomen and others who had left good cellars for the veldt. The old knack came back to us both, though I believe that I alone was conscious of it at the time; and we were leaving the house, splendidly supplied, when we almost ran into the arms of an infantry officer, with a scowl upon his red-hot face, and an eye-glass flaming at us in the sun.

"Peter Bellingham!" gasped Raffles under his breath, and then we saluted and tried to pass on, with the bottles ringing like church-bells under our khaki. But Captain Bellingham was a hard man.

"What have you men been doin'?" drawled he.

"Nothing, sir," we protested, like innocence with an injury.

"Lootin' 's forbidden," said he. "You had better let me see those bottles."

"We are done," whispered Raffles, and straightway we made a sideboard of the stoop across which he had crept at so inopportune a moment. I had not the heart to raise my eyes again, yet it was many moments before the officer broke silence.

"Uam Var!" he murmured reverentially at last. "And Long John of Ben Nevis! The first drop that's been discovered in the whole psalm-singing show! What lot do you two belong to?"

I answered.

　　　　　　　　　　　　　　　　　　　　　　　　E.W. HORNUNG

"I must have your names."

In my agitation I gave my real one. Raffles had turned away, as though in heart-broken contemplation of our lost loot. I saw the officer studying his half-profile with an alarming face.

"What's YOUR name?" he rapped out at last.

But his strange, low voice said plainly that he knew, and Raffles faced him with the monosyllable of confession and assent. I did not count the seconds until the next word, but it was Captain Bellingham who uttered it at last.

"I thought you were dead."

"Now you see I am not."

"But you are at your old games!"

"I am not," cried Raffles, and his tone was new to me. I have seldom heard one more indignant. "Yes," he continued, "this is loot, and the wrong 'un will out. That's what you're thinking, Peter—I beg your pardon—sir. But he isn't let out in the field! We're playing the game as much as you are, old—sir."

The plural number caused the captain to toss me a contemptuous look. "Is this the fellah who was taken when you swam for it?" he inquired, relapsing into his drawl. Raffles said I was, and with that took a passionate oath upon our absolute rectitude as volunteers. There could be no doubting him; but the officer's eyes went back at the bottles on the stoop.

"But look at those," said he; and as he looked himself the light eye melted in his fiery face. "And I've got Sparklets in my tent," he sighed. "You make it in a minute!"

Not a word from Raffles, and none, you may be sure, from me. Then suddenly Bellingham told me where his tent was, and, adding that our case was one for serious consideration, strode in its direction without another word until some sunlit paces separated us.

"You can bring that stuff with you," he then flung over a shoulder-strap, "and I advise you to put it where you had it before."

A trooper saluted him some yards further on, and looked evilly at us as we followed with our loot. It was Corporal Connal of ours, and the thought of him takes my mind off the certainly gallant captain who only that day had joined our division with the reinforcements. I could not stand the man myself. He added soda-water to our whiskey in his tent, and would only keep a couple of bottles when we came away. Softened by the spirit, to which disuse made us all a little sensitive, our officer was soon convinced of the honest part that we were playing for once, and for fifty minutes of the hour we spent with him he and Raffles talked cricket without a break. On parting they even shook hands; that was Long John in the captain's head; but the snob never addressed a syllable to me.

And now to the gallows-bird who was still corporal of our troop: it was not long before Raffles was to have his wish and the traitor's wicket. We had resumed our advance, or rather our humble part in the great surrounding movement then taking place, and were under pretty heavy fire once more, when Connal was shot in the hand. It was a curious casualty in more than one respect, and nobody seems to have seen it happen. Though a flesh wound, it was a bloody one, and that may be why the surgeon did not at once detect those features which afterwards convinced him that the injury had been self-inflicted. It was the right hand, and until it healed the man could be of no further use in the firing line; nor was the case serious enough for admission to a crowded field-hospital; and Connal himself offered his services as custodian of a number of our horses which we were keeping out of harm's way in a donga. They had come there in the following manner: That morning we had been heliographed to reinforce the C.M.R., only to find that the enemy had the range to a nicety when we reached the spot. There were trenches for us men, but no place of safety for our horses nearer than this long and narrow donga which ran from within our lines towards those of the Boers. So some of us galloped them thither, six-in-hand, amid the whine of shrapnel and the whistle of shot. I remember the man next me being killed by a shell with all his team, and the tangle of flying harness, torn horseflesh, and crimson khaki, that we left behind us on the veldt; also that a small red flag, ludicrously like those used to indicate a putting-green, marked the single sloping entrance to the otherwise precipitous donga, which I for one was duly thankful to reach alive.

The same evening Connal, with a few other light casualties to assist him, took over the charge for which he had volunteered and for which he was so admirably fitted by his knowledge of horses and his general experience of the country; nevertheless, he managed to lose three or four fine chargers in the course of the first night; and, early in the second, Raffles shook me out of a heavy slumber in the trenches where we had been firing all day.

"I have found the spot, Bunny," he whispered; "we ought to out him before the night is over."

"Connal?"

Raffles nodded.

"You know what happened to some of his horses last night? Well, he let them go himself."

"Never!"

"I'm as certain of it," said Raffles, "as though I'd seen him do it; and if he does it again I shall see him. I can even tell you how it happened. Connal insisted on having one end of the donga to himself, and of course his end is the one nearest the Boers. Well, then, he tells the other fellows to go to sleep at their end—I have it direct from one of them—and you bet they don't need a second invitation. The rest I hope to see to-night."

"It seems almost incredible," said I.

"Not more so than the Light Horseman's dodge of poisoning the troughs; that happened at Ladysmith before Christmas; and two kind friends did for that blackguard what you and I are going to do for this one, and a firing-party did the rest. Brutes! A mounted man's worth a file on foot in this country, and well they know it. But this beauty goes one better than the poison; that was wilful waste; but I'll eat my wideawake if our loss last night wasn't the enemy's double gain! What we've got to do, Bunny, is to catch him in the act. It may mean watching him all night, but was ever game so well worth the candle?"

One may say in passing that, at this particular point of contact, the enemy were in superior force, and for once in a mood as aggressive as our own. They were led with a dash, and handled with a skill, which did not always characterize their commanders at this stage of the war. Their position was very similar to ours, and indeed we were to spend the whole of next day in trying with an equal will to turn each other out. The result will scarcely be forgotten by those who recognize the occasion from these remarks. Meanwhile it was the eve of battle (most evenings were), and there was that villain with the horses in the donga, and here were we two upon his track.

Raffles's plan was to reconnoitre the place, and then take up a position from which we could watch our man and pounce upon him if he gave us cause. The spot that we eventually chose and stealthily occupied was behind some bushes through which we could see down into the donga; there were the precious horses; and there sure enough was our wounded corporal, sitting smoking in his cloak, some glimmering thing in his lap.

"That's his revolver, and it's a Mauser," whispered Raffles. "He shan't have a chance of using it on us; either we must be on him before he knows we are anywhere near, or simply report. It's easily proved once we are sure; but I should like to have the taking of him too."

There was a setting moon. Shadows were sharp and black. The man smoked steadily, and the hungry horses did what I never saw horses do before; they stood and nibbled at each other's tails. I was used to sleeping in the open, under the jewelled dome that seems so much vaster and grander in these wide spaces of the earth. I lay listening to the horses, and to the myriad small strange voices of the veldt, to which I cannot even now put a name, while Raffles watched. "One head is better than two," he said, "when you don't want it to be seen." We were to take watch and watch about, however, and the other might sleep if he could; it was not my fault that I did nothing else; it was Raffles who could trust nobody but himself. Nor was there any time for recriminations when he did rouse me in the end.

But a moment ago, as it seemed to me, I had been gazing upward at the stars and listening to the dear, minute sounds of peace; and in another the great gray slate was clean, and every bone of me set in plaster of Paris, and sniping beginning between pickets with the day. It was an occasional crack, not a constant crackle, but the whistle of a bullet as it passed us by, or a tiny transitory flame for the one bit of detail on a blue hill-side, was an unpleasant warning that we two on ours were a target in ourselves. But Raffles paid no attention to their fire; he was pointing downward through the bushes to where Corporal Connal stood with his back to us, shooing a last charger out of the mouth of the donga towards the Boer trenches.

"That's his third," whispered Raffles, "but it's the first I've seen distinctly, for he waited for the blind spot before the dawn. It's enough to land him, I fancy, but we mustn't lose time. Are you ready for a creep?"

I stretched myself, and said I was; but I devoutly wished it was not quite so early in the morning.

"Like cats, then, till he hears, and then into him for all we're worth. He's stowed his iron safe away, but he mustn't have time even to feel for it. You take his left arm, Bunny, and hang on to that like a ferret, and I'll do the rest. Ready? Then now!"

And in less time than it would take to tell, we were over the lip of the donga and had fallen upon the fellow before he could turn his head; nevertheless, for a few instants he fought like a wild beast, striking,

E.W. HORNUNG

kicking, and swinging me off my feet as I obeyed my instructions to the letter, and stuck to his left like a leech. But he soon gave that up, panting and blaspheming, demanded explanations in his hybrid tongue that had half a brogue and half a burr. What were we doing? What had he done? Raffles at his back, with his right wrist twisted round and pinned into the small of it, soon told him that, and I think the words must have been the first intimation that he had as to who his assailants were.

"So it's you two!" he cried, and a light broke over him. He was no longer trying to shake us off, and now he dropped his curses also, and stood chuckling to himself instead. "Well," he went on, "you're bloody liars both, but I know something else that you are, so you'd better let go."

A coldness ran through me, and I never saw Raffles so taken aback. His grip must have relaxed for a fraction of time, for our captive broke out in a fresh and desperate struggle, but now we pinned him tighter than ever, and soon I saw him turning green and yellow with the pain.

"You're breaking my wrist!" he yelled at last.

"Then stand still and tell us who we are."

And he stood still and told us our real names. But Raffles insisted on hearing how he had found us out, and smiled as though he had known what was coming when it came. I was dumbfounded.

The accursed hound had followed us that evening to Captain Bellingham's tent, and his undoubted cleverness in his own profession of spy had done the rest.

"And now you'd better let me go," said the master of the situation, as I for one could not help regarding him.

"I'll see you damned," said Raffles, savagely.

"Then you're damned and done for yourself, my cocky criminal. Raffles the burglar! Raffles the society thief! Not dead after all, but 'live and 'listed. Send him home and give him fourteen years, and won't he like 'em, that's all!"

"I shall have the pleasure of hearing you shot first," retorted Raffles, through his teeth, "and that alone will make them bearable. Come on, Bunny, let's drive the swine along and get it over."

And drive him we did, he cursing, cajoling, struggling, gloating, and blubbering by turns. But Raffles never wavered for an instant, though his face was tragic, and it went to my heart, where that look stays still. I remember at the time, though I never let my hold relax, there was a moment when I added my entreaties to those of our prisoner. Raffles did not even reply to me. But I was thinking of him, I swear. I was thinking of that gray set face that I never saw before or after.

"Your story will be tested," said the commanding officer, when Connal had been marched to the guard-tent. "Is there any truth in his?"

"It is perfectly true, sir."

"And the notorious Raffles has been alive all these years, and you are really he?"

"I am, sir."

"And what are you doing at the front?"

Somehow I thought that Raffles was going to smile, but the grim set of his mouth never altered, neither was there any change in the ashy pallor which had come over him in the donga when Connal mouthed his name. It was only his eyes that lighted up at the last question.

"I am fighting, sir," said he, as simply as any subaltern in the army.

The commanding officer inclined a grizzled head perceptibly, and no more. He was not one of any school, our General; he had his own ways, and we loved both him and them; and I believe that he loved the rough but gallant corps that bore his name. He once told us that he knew something about most of us, and there were things that Raffles had done of which he must have heard. But he only moved his grizzled head.

"Did you know he was going to give you away?" he asked at length, with a jerk of it toward the guard-tent.

"Yes, sir."

"But you thought it worth while, did you?"

"I thought it necessary, sir."

The General paused, drumming on his table, making up his mind. Then his chin came up with the decision that we loved in him.

"I shall sift all this," said he. "An officer's name was mentioned, and I shall see him myself. Meanwhile you had better go on—fighting."

IV

Corporal Connal paid the penalty of his crime before the sun was far above the hill held by the enemy. There was abundance of circumstantial evidence against him, besides the direct testimony of Raffles and myself, and the wretch was shot at last with little ceremony and less shrift. And that was the one good thing that happened on the day that broke upon us hiding behind the bushes overlooking the donga; by noon it was my own turn.

I have avoided speaking of my wound before I need, and from the preceding pages you would not gather that I am more or less lame for life. You will soon see now why I was in no hurry to recall the incident. I used to think of a wound received in one's country's service as the proudest trophy a man could acquire. But the sight of mine depresses me every morning of my life; it was due for one thing to my own slow eye for cover, in taking which (to aggravate my case) our hardy little corps happened to excel.

The bullet went clean through my thigh, drilling the bone, but happily missing the sciatic nerve; thus the mere pain was less than it might have been, but of course I went over in a light-brown heap. We were advancing on our stomachs to take the hill, and thus extend our position, and it was at this point that the fire became too heavy for us, so that for hours (in the event) we moved neither forward nor back. But it was not a minute before Raffles came to me through the whistling scud, and in another I was on my back behind a shallow rock, with him kneeling over me and unrolling my bandage in the teeth of that murderous fire. It was on the knees of the gods, he said, when I begged him to bend lower, but for the moment I thought his tone as changed as his face had been earlier in the morning. To oblige me, however, he took more care; and, when he had done all that one comrade could for another, he did avail himself of the cover he had found for me. So there we lay together on the veldt, under blinding sun and withering fire, and I suppose it is the veldt that I should describe, as it swims and flickers before wounded eyes. I shut mine to bring it back, but all that comes is the keen brown face of Raffles, still a shade paler than its wont; now bending to sight and fire; now peering to see results, brows raised, eyes widened; anon turning to me with the word to set my tight lips grinning. He was talking all the time, but for my sake, and I knew it. Can you wonder that I could not see an inch beyond him? He was the battle to me then; he is the whole war to me as I look back now.

"Feel equal to a cigarette? It will buck you up, Bunny. No, that one in the silver paper, I've hoarded it for this. Here's a light; and so Bunny takes the Sullivan! All honor to the sporting rabbit!"

"At least I went over like one," said I, sending the only clouds into the blue, and chiefly wishing for their longer endurance. I was as hot as a cinder from my head to one foot; the other leg was ceasing to belong to me.

"Wait a bit," says Raffles, puckering; "there's a gray felt hat at deep long-on, and I want to add it to the bag for vengeance. . . Wait—yes—no, no luck! I must pitch 'em up a bit more. Hallo! Magazine empty. How goes the Sullivan, Bunny? Rum to be smoking one on the veldt with a hole in your leg!"

"It's doing me good," I said, and I believe it was. But Raffles lay looking at me as he lightened his bandolier.

"Do you remember," he said softly, "the day we first began to think about the war? I can see the pink, misty river light, and feel the first bite there was in the air when one stood about; don't you wish we had either here! 'Orful slorter, orful slorter;' that fellow's face, I see it too; and here we have the thing he cried. Can you believe it's only six months ago?"

"Yes," I sighed, enjoying the thought of that afternoon less than he did; "yes, we were slow to catch fire at first."

"Too slow," he said quickly.

"But when we did catch," I went on, wishing we never had, "we soon burnt up."

"And then went out," laughed Raffles gayly. He was loaded up again. "Another over at the gray felt hat," said he; "by Jove, though, I believe he's having an over at me!"

"I wish you'd be careful," I urged. "I heard it too."

"My dear Bunny, it's on the knees you wot of. If anything's down in the specifications surely that is. Besides—that was nearer!"

"To you?"

"No, to him. Poor devil, he has his specifications too; it's comforting to think that. . . I can't see where that one pitched; it may have been a wide; and it's very nearly the end of the over again. Feeling worse, Bunny?"

"No, I've only closed my eyes. Go on talking."

"It was I who let you in for this," he said, at his bandolier again.

"No, I'm glad I came out."

And I believe I still was, in a way; for it WAS rather fine to be wounded, just then, with the pain growing less; but the sensation was not to last me many minutes, and I can truthfully say that I have never felt it since.

"Ah, but you haven't had such a good time as I have!"

"Perhaps not."

Had his voice vibrated, or had I imagined it? Pain-waves and loss of blood were playing tricks with my senses; now they were quite dull, and my leg alive and throbbing; now I had no leg at all, but more than all my ordinary senses in every other part of me. And the devil's orchestra was playing all the time, and all around me, on every class of fiendish instrument, which you have been made to hear for yourselves in every newspaper. Yet all that I heard was Raffles talking.

"I have had a good time, Bunny."

Yes, his voice was sad; but that was all; the vibration must have been in me.

"I know you have, old chap," said I.

"I am grateful to the General for giving me to-day. It may be the last. Then I can only say it's been the best—by Jove!"

"What is it?"

And I opened my eyes. His were shining. I can see them now.

"Got him—got the hat! No, I'm hanged if I have; at least he wasn't in it. The crafty cuss, he must have stuck it up on purpose. Another over. . . scoring's slow. . . I wonder if he's sportsman enough to take a hint? His hat-trick's foolish. Will he show his face if I show mine?"

I lay with closed ears and eyes. My leg had come to life again, and the rest of me was numb.

"Bunny!"

His voice sounded higher. He must have been sitting upright.

"Well?"

But it was not well with me; that was all I thought as my lips made the word.

"It's not only been the best time I ever had, old Bunny, but I'm not half sure—"

Of what I can but guess; the sentence was not finished, and never could be in this world.

A Note About the Author

Ernest William Hornung (1866–1921) was an English author and poet, best known as a crime writer who often published under his initials, E.W. Hornung. When he was seventeen, Hornung moved to Australia, with the hope that the climate would remedy his poor health. Hornung often referred to this time as one of the best periods of his life, and he based much of his work off an Australian setting. A little over two years later, Hornung returned to England and worked as a journalist during the active period of the infamous serial killer Jack the Ripper, which likely sparked his interest in crime fiction. Hornung married Connie Doyle, the sister of major author Arthur Conan Doyle, in 1893. While the author explored many important themes in his work, the topics of Australia, crime, and cricket were commonly present in his work, signifying Hornung's interest and passion for each.

A Note from the Publisher

Spanning many genres, from non-fiction essays to literature classics to children's books and lyric poetry, Mint Edition books showcase the master works of our time in a modern new package. The text is freshly typeset, is clean and easy to read, and features a new note about the author in each volume. Many books also include exclusive new introductory material. Every book boasts a striking new cover, which makes it as appropriate for collecting as it is for gift giving. Mint Edition books are only printed when a reader orders them, so natural resources are not wasted. We're proud that our books are never manufactured in excess and exist only in the exact quantity they need to be read and enjoyed.

Discover more of your favorite classics with Bookfinity™.

- Track your reading with custom book lists.
- Get great book recommendations for your personalized Reader Type.
- Add reviews for your favorite books.
- AND MUCH MORE!

Visit **bookfinity.com** and take the fun Reader Type quiz to get started.

Enjoy our classic and modern companion pairings!